Abiga
Ertle's
Book

Baby-sitters' Fright Night

**Other books by
Ann M. Martin**

Rachel Parker, Kindergarten Show-off
Eleven Kids, One Summer
Ma and Pa Dracula
Yours Turly, Shirley
Ten Kids, No Pets
Slam Book
Just a Summer Romance
Missing Since Monday
With You and Without You
Me and Katie (the Pest)
Stage Fright
Inside Out
Bummer Summer

BABY-SITTERS LITTLE SISTER series
THE BABY-SITTERS CLUB mysteries
THE BABY-SITTERS CLUB series

Baby-sitters' Fright Night

Ann M. Martin

An
APPLE
PAPERBACK

SCHOLASTIC INC.
New York Toronto London Auckland Sydney

The author gratefully acknowledges
Nola Thacker
for her help in
preparing this manuscript.

Cover art by Hodges Soileau

ISBN 0-590-69180-5

12 11 10 9 8 7 6 5 4 3   8 9/9 0 1/0

Printed in the U.S.A.

First Scholastic printing, October 1996

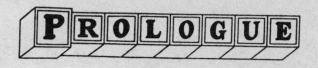

PROLOGUE

How did it happen? How did I become caught up in the scariest Halloween of my life? I mean, Halloween is kid stuff. It's little devils and little witches and little princesses and little ninja turtles having their pictures taken, shouting "trick or treat," pigging out on candy, and being hyperactive from the sugar rush the next day. As a professional baby-sitter, I can tell you that it is not my favorite holiday, based on the candy factor alone. Plus a lot of

older kids use
Halloween as an
excuse to go out and
do really dumb or
even mean things.
They are the biggest
babies of all.

So how did it
happen? I suppose
I could blame the
Baby-sitters Club, or
BSC, which I innocently
joined when I moved
to Stoneybrook, Con-
necticut, not too long
ago. You might have
heard of the Baby-
sitters Club. If you
haven't, you'll hear
more about it in a
little while.

But it wasn't really
the fault of the BSC.
After all, it wasn't the
club's plan to take a
Halloween trip to Salem,
Massachusetts. That
was the brilliant idea
of Stoneybrook middle

school. What better place to spend an educational Halloween weekend than Salem, where people were hanged as witches in the 1700s?

Not exactly my dream vacation. But then, the last trip I took with the BSC turned out to be a fright trip after all, parts of which still scare me.

I wasn't thinking about that ski trip, though, or the mystery we'd been involved in, when SMS announced the trip to Salem. I just signed up and started making plans.

As it turned out, I should have made plans for another mystery. A mystery involving witches and curses and... well, let

3

me just put it this
way:
     The trip to Salem
for Halloween turned
out to be a real
scream.

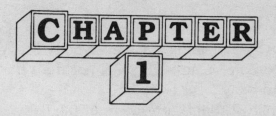

CHAPTER 1

Abby

Wednesday

Chaos reigned at the last meeting of the BSC before we left on our trip to Salem. Of course, since Kristy was in charge, it was organized chaos. Sort of.

Abby

"Where is everybody? Mary Anne, do you have the notebook? Has everybody brought it up to date? Dues — no, it's not dues day. It's Wednesday."

Kristy Thomas, president of the Baby-sitters Club, was in what my mother calls a "tizzy." We were leaving for the Halloween retreat to Salem the next morning, and Kristy was preparing to leave someone else in charge of the BSC.

"Wonderful Wednesday," I said, closing the door of Claudia Kishi's room behind me.

"Abby," said Kristy, checking her watch. "You're —"

"Right on time. Take it easy, Madame President. We're only going to be gone four days. What could happen in four days?" (The answer to that question, in case you're interested, is *lots*. But I didn't know that then.)

Mary Anne Spier, who is the secretary of the BSC, held up the club notebook. "I have the notebook, which I am about to hand to Mallory for her update. I have the record book. So quit worrying."

The phone rang. Kristy shrieked, "The phone! Where is the phone?"

"Where it always is, Kristy." Claudia, who'd been delicately picking all the yellow M & Ms out of a giant bag, reached out and scooped up the receiver. "Baby-sitters Club," she said. She asked some questions, scribbled a few notes, and hung up. "The Hobarts," she announced. "For Sunday afternoon."

Kristy said, "Oh, no. We only have four baby-sitters on call. What if —"

Calmly, Mary Anne flipped open the record book. "Shannon? Or Jessi? Oops, not Jessi."

With a grin, Jessi Ramsey bowed in Shannon Kilbourne's direction. Jessi is a ballet dancer, and she had a part in Stoneybrook University's Halloween Dance performance. "You're it, Shannon," Jessi said.

"Fine by me," Shannon answered. Mary Anne wrote down the details of the job in the record book, while Claudia called the Hobarts back to confirm.

Kristy calmed down, at least momentarily, and we handled a few more phone calls. Claudia's bedroom, where we hold our meetings, was packed to overflowing. Not only were the seven regular members of the BSC present, but our two associate members were also present — at Kristy's special request. Since five of us would be away for *four whole days*, she wanted everybody at the meeting.

This was so that, Kristy-style, she could double- and triple-check every detail, and make plans for everything that might go wrong. As

7

the meeting progressed, she peppered Jessi, Claudia, Shannon, and Logan Bruno with questions: Did everyone have their Kid-Kits? Were they up-to-date with the club notebook? (Yes and yes, and more about the Kid-Kits later.)

Suddenly, Mallory Pike held out her hands toward Kristy, closed her eyes, and intoned, "Calm. You will be calm." She wriggled her fingers and twitched her nose.

Kristy burst out laughing. "What are you doing, Mal?"

With a grin, Mal opened her eyes. "Jordan says he has discovered an ancient book of secret spells. He won't let anybody see it, but he claims he's been putting spells on Adam and Byron." Jordan, Adam, and Byron Pike are ten-year-old triplets, younger brothers of Mallory, who is the oldest of eight siblings. Triplets mean triple fun — and triple trouble. As Mal has said more than once (sometimes proudly and sometimes in despair), in a family as big as hers, there is never a dull moment.

"I wish spells really worked," said Claudia. "I'd like to put a spell on my homework. Except," she added darkly, "I think it is already bewitched."

"Maybe we can find something in Salem to help you out. After all, the advertisements call it a 'bewitching city,'" said Mary Anne.

"Salem's not just about witches, you know," said Stacey McGill unexpectedly. "I mean, America's first millionaire lived there. And his money came from shipping and trade. Salem used to be an important seaport and the sixth largest town in America."

Claudia held up her hands. "Stop! You sound like a book report. I'd forgotten this trip was a school project and you were going to have to do homework about it. Maybe I should be glad my parents are too worried about my grades to let me go."

"Reports or no reports, I wish our school would plan a trip like that for us," said Shannon. Shannon goes to a private school, which is why she wasn't coming on the trip with us. She is one of the associate members of the BSC, and doesn't come to meetings regularly the way the rest of us do.

Logan is our other associate member. He's a great baby-sitter and, even more excellently, someone who will play any sport, any time, anywhere. Logan had said no to the trip because of a big football game that weekend. He's on the SMS football team (and the track team, and the volleyball team, and the baseball team, too).

Kristy said, "The phone number for the inn is listed in information, if you lose it. You just call information for Salem, Massachusetts."

Abby

"1-800-W-I-T-C-H," I cracked. "Seriously, folks," I continued, as everyone groaned. "Have you taken a look at any of the books on Salem that the teachers have been handing around? There are at least three museums about witches, including a wax museum!"

"I hope they aren't too scary," Mary Anne said. "I'd like to take Nidia to some of them. I think she would have fun."

Nidia is the daughter of Ms. Garcia, who was one of the chaperons for the trip, along with Coach Wu (everyone calls her that, even though she teaches social studies as well as coaches the girls' softball team), Mr. Blake, and Mrs. Bernhardt. Mrs. Bernhardt also teaches social studies. *Mrs.* Blake and *Mr.* Wu were coming up to join us that weekend, too. Twenty kids, at least four chaperons . . . and how many witches?

Anyway, Ms. Garcia had asked if anyone in the BSC wanted a sitting job during the trip, and Mary Anne had volunteered.

"Yeah, you better not scare a teacher's kid," I warned Mary Anne. "You don't know what that would do to your grade point average."

Reaching down into the briefcase that she carries instead of a backpack these days, Mallory produced a guidebook to Salem and flipped it open. After studying it for a minute or two she announced, "No problem, Mary Anne. The

wax museum sounds pretty tame. It has inter-
active displays. You can even make tombstone
rubbings."

"If I were going to Salem," said Claudia, "I
could use that as the basis for my Salem report.
A collage of Salem. That wouldn't be so bad."

I felt sorry for Claudia. So did soft-hearted
Mary Anne, only, unlike me, Mary Anne was
quick to show it. "I'll make you a tombstone
rubbing, Claudia."

"And there is going to be at least one parade,
probably more than one." Mallory jumped back
into the conversation, still intent on her guidebook. "In Salem, they have a whole celebration
around Halloween called Haunted Happenings. Haunted houses, guided mystery tours,
costume balls."

The phone rang. As Claudia picked it up, Logan said, "See, Kristy? Nothing's going to happen here in Stoneybrook. Salem is where all the
action is going to be. So quit worrying."

Kristy

Thursday

nothing will go wrong, nothing will go wrong, nothing will go wrong. That's what the wheels of the bus taking us from Stoneybrook to Salem kept saying — in between saying nothing will go right, nothing will go right, nothing will go right....

Logan, Shannon, Claud, and Jessi had told me not to worry, and I knew they were right. After all, it was insulting of me to think that my fellow BSC members couldn't handle club business just because I wasn't around. They'd done it before.

But I was still worrying the next afternoon as the bus groaned out of the Stoneybrook Middle School parking lot.

Abby leaned across the aisle and gave my arm a friendly punch. "Hey, this beats the Wheeze Wagon, doesn't it?" The Wheeze Wagon is what Abby calls our school bus (she and I are neighbors).

I nodded, barely registering what should have been a very noticeable lack of coughing and lurching on the part of the bus, not to mention the fact that the seats and floors were actually free of gum, the corpses of former spitballs, broken pens, smashed bits of dropped lunches, and other disgusting things that I happen to believe are recycled from the school bus floor directly into our school lunches.

"Yo, Thomas," said Abby. "Snap out of it!"

Mary Anne, who was sitting next to me, put a sympathetic hand on my arm. "Kristy, you know worrying isn't going to change anything."

I sighed. "True. And once we're in Salem, I

will snap out of it. I'm sure we'll have so much to do that I won't have time to worry. So I might as well get it over with now, right?"

Mal's head popped over the seat in front of us, and she dropped one of her guidebooks in Mary Anne's lap.

"Thanks," said Mary Anne.

"I've got dibs on it after you," said Stacey, who was sitting across the aisle from Mal. "I just had an idea for my Salem project — something on its early economic history."

Typical Stacey, I thought. She's a math whiz, and numbers (and economics) are her thing. She wants to be the head of a small company some-day, but I don't think she will be. It's more likely to be a major corporation.

Meanwhile, her head for numbers is the rea-son she is the treasurer of the BSC, the same way my talent for leadership and organization (not to mention the fact that the BSC was my idea) is the reason I'm the president. And the level-headed way I handle myself in a crisis.

Like the one that happened as I sank deeper into my worry-and-brood mode.

Something cold and slimy and disgusting and icky touched my neck and then wriggled beneath the collar of my shirt and down my spine.

Snakes, I thought wildly. Worms. Not that I

am afraid of snakes or worms or anything like that, but I do *not* want to share my shirt space with them.

I didn't say that of course. In spite of myself, what I said was, *"Eeeeek!"* I jumped to my feet. At that moment, the bus took a turn and I lost my balance and fell back across Mary Anne.

Snickers and laughter broke out behind me. "Alan Gray," I said through gritted teeth as Mary Anne helped me up. "You are dead meat."

Alan Gray is, without question, the biggest jerk in the eighth grade. Even if he were in second grade, he'd be the biggest jerk, but at least there his tricks would be age-appropriate. What had I done to deserve this? Nothing that I could think of. But Alan has never needed a reason to be jerky.

"Here, I'll get it." Mary Anne stuck her hand inside the collar of my shirt and in one deft move pulled out something long and white and cold and icky.

"Spaghetti for Kristy, special delivery," sang Alan, and laughed even harder at his stupid trick.

I saw Cary Retlin watching, a little smile on his lips. Cary Retlin is sort of my nemesis in the class. He is a world-class prank player and (I suspect) the leader of a group of prank players who call themselves the Mischief Knights. Cary and I have had run-ins before. We even faced off in a mystery challenge once.

But Cary's style doesn't include babyish things such as dropping cold spaghetti down someone's back.

He said now, "It's chilled, Kristy. An Alan Gray special touch."

I snatched the spaghetti from Mary Anne and hurled it at Alan. "You touch me again, spaghetti-brain, and you're going to wish *you* were frozen!"

Fuming, I sat down again. How had I overlooked the fact that both Alan Gray *and* Cary Retlin were on this little Halloween jaunt? Trouble, trouble, everywhere, I thought glumly.

And more trouble.

"Alan, give the spaghetti to Eileen. Maybe she can cast a spell on it and turn it into a worm. After all, she did say one of her ancestors was tried in Salem for being a witch," Cokie Mason's unpleasant voice called out.

More snickers.

In the grand tradition of cowardly bullies everywhere, Cokie Mason, student at SMS most likely to succeed at being hated by everyone with brains or heart, had decided to pick on someone weaker: Eileen Murphy. Not only was Eileen at an age disadvantage, since she is a sixth-grader and Cokie is an eighth-grader, but

Eileen has not yet developed any, well, social skills. She ducks her head when she talks to you, never looking you directly in the eye. Or she stares at you intensely, making you uneasy. She probably was telling the truth about having had an ancestor tried as a witch. But if you're going to go around telling people things like that, you have to be prepared to be teased, and to give as good as you get if you don't want to be teased forever.

Eileen gulped and ducked and stammered and insisted that she wasn't a witch. Not the most effective response.

Especially since her fashion sense appeared to be about on par with her social skills: She was wearing a big, loose, dingy, black outfit — making her look a little bit like the stereotypical pictures of witches on broomsticks.

Then I heard the voice of Cokie's sidekick, Grace Blume. "Yeah, Eileen, go on. Show us how a real witch acts."

Laughter now. "I'm not a witch," said a small, intense voice.

"Yeah," said Alan Gray, "leave her alone."

Good for Alan, I thought, surprised. But his next words spoiled the effect. "Eileen didn't even bring her broomstick!"

Abby had straightened in her seat, an angry spark in her eye. I was taking a deep breath, about to let Cokie have it, but just then Ms. Garcia, demonstrating the sixth sense that some teachers have, stood up and looked back over the bus.

"We're almost there, everybody. Don't stand up, but please do start getting organized."

Cokie made a dive for her purse and pulled out a mirror and some lipstick. Grace did the same. I sourly hoped that the mirrors would crack, but of course they didn't.

Alan oozed down in his seat when Ms. Garcia sent a sharp glance in his direction.

Eileen turned her face to the window, and the moment passed.

But I continued to brood.

Trouble, I thought. Trouble.

CHAPTER 3

Mary Anne

Thursday

I could tell Kristy was
worrying, but I couldn't
think of any way to help
her out. Being president
of the BSC is a big respons-
ibility. After all, we are
a growing business. As
Stacey would point out,
our staff has more than
doubled since we started,
not so long ago.

Mary Anne

But I'd better begin at the beginning. Since Kristy is the president and founder of the BSC, as well as being one of my two best friends, I'll start with her.

Kristy is thirteen years old and an eighth-grader at Stoneybrook Middle School, like most of the members of the BSC. Kristy's family is a very large and blended one: three adults — her mother; her stepfather, Watson Brewer; and her maternal grandmother, Nannie — and seven children. The children are Kristy; her two older brothers, Charlie and Sam; her seven-year-old brother, David Michael; her adopted baby sister, Emily Michelle, who was born in Vietnam; her stepsister Karen, who is seven; and her step-brother Andrew, who is four. (Karen and Andrew are Watson's children from his first marriage. They live at Kristy's house part-time.) She also has one puppy, Shannon, a Bernese Mountain dog; one cranky cat, Boo-Boo; other assorted smaller pets; and one ghost (at least, that's what Karen insists — that the ghost of one of Watson's ancestors, Ben Brewer, lives in his own room on the third floor).

Fortunately, Kristy lives in a mansion, so there is room enough for everyone, even the ghost of Ben Brewer. But before her mom married Watson, the five Thomases lived in a house that was pretty small for three boys and one girl and one adult. (That house was next door to my old one, and across the street from Claudia Kishi's.) Mr. Thomas lived there for awhile, too, but he left when David Michael was a baby.

So Kristy had to learn to be organized and responsible early on, which is one of the reasons she's a good baby-sitter and a good club president.

Another reason she is the perfect BSC president is that the club was her idea. You might say that David Michael is the reason that the BSC exists. Kristy came up with the idea for the club one afternoon as she listened to her mother call one sitter after another, trying to find a baby-sitter for David Michael. If only she could just dial one number and reach several sitters at once, Kristy thought.

And that's how it all started.

It was clearly an idea whose time had come, because now, not much later, we have all the baby-sitting jobs we can handle, even with seven regular members and two associates. We almost never have to hand out fliers or put up signs to advertise the way we did in the beginning. Most of our business comes from satisfied customers who tell other parents about us.

We meet every Monday, Wednesday, and Friday from five-thirty to six. Clients know they

MaryAnne

can reach us then to set up baby-sitting jobs. We meet in Claudia's room because she has her own phone line. That way we don't tie up someone else's phone. Claudia is the BSC's vice-president.

I am the club secretary and am responsible for keeping all the appointments in the club record book. That way we never forget who is supposed to be baby-sitting where, or who can't take a job because of a prior commitment. I don't mean to brag, but I have never, ever made a scheduling mistake, and I do a good job of keeping the record book (which also has a list of all of our clients' names, addresses, and phone numbers, plus other important information) up-to-date.

We also keep a club notebook. In it, we write up every single baby-sitting job we go on. And we all read the notebook at least once a week. That way, we keep up with our clients — who has developed an allergy to peanut butter, for example, or who is in a practical-joke phase.

A third volume recently joined our BSC bookshelf: the mystery notebook. Kristy started that when we were being stalked by this maniac while we were snowed in . . . well, I won't go into that here. But we realized that we have been in the middle of quite a few mysteries, and

22

we needed a central place in which to keep track of our clues and solutions. So Mal dug through the club notebook and wrote up everything she could find about our previous mysteries. If we ever run into another mystery, we'll know where to put our notes.

Each of us keeps something else that makes for better baby-sitting: a Kid-Kit. That's Kristy's fun name for yet another simple but brilliant idea. Kid-Kits are boxes filled with old toys, games, books, and puzzles, plus markers, stickers, and whatever else we can think of. We all decorated our boxes, and we change the contents from time to time. On rainy days, or when we have a difficult baby-sitting job ahead — such as a kid who has been in bed a long time with a cold and is really cranky — we take our kits along as a special treat. This works. Guaranteed.

I have to say, though, that the real key to the Baby-sitters Club's success is . . . the baby-sitters! So here's a little more about the rest of us.

In some ways, Kristy and I are alike. We've been best friends since we were practically babies. We are both short and have brown hair and brown eyes and are fairly conventional fashion-wise. (Although Kristy's unvarying preference for jeans and a T-shirt or turtleneck has led some people to refer to her look as a "uniform," while mine covers a wider range of preppy territory, I guess.)

And like Kristy, I have a blended family, although a much smaller one. I used to be an only child with an only parent; my mother died when I was a baby and my father raised me himself. He was very, very strict. He chose all my clothes and even my hairstyle — pigtails — until recently. That was fine when I was little, but not so fine as I grew older. Dad didn't realize that the time had come to let me be more responsible about a lot of things, including choosing my own wardrobe. It took some work, but I convinced him to relax a little.

And he became even more laid-back (for Dad) when Dawn Schafer and her family moved to Stoneybrook from California.

What do I mean by that? Well, Dawn's mother had grown up in Stoneybrook, and she and my father had been high-school sweethearts. When Dawn (who had become my other best friend as well as a BSC member) and I found out about the old romance, we helped rekindle it. The next thing we knew, my dad and Dawn's mom were getting married!

So Dad and I and my kitten Tigger moved into the Schafers' old farmhouse on the edge of town — a farmhouse with a secret passage and, Dawn believes, a ghost.

Another trait I share with Kristy is a love of organization. But while Kristy is a firm believer in the adage "the squeaky wheel gets the grease" and does not hesitate to express her opinions loudly and often (some people have been known to call her bossy), I am shy and sensitive. In spite of myself, I cry easily and I am very soft-hearted. And while Kristy is good at talking, I am good at listening.

I am also the first member of the BSC to have a boyfriend: Logan, one of our associate members. More about him in just a minute.

Right now, you should know a little more about Dawn, because she is still important to the BSC as well as to me. After all, she is still my sister and one of my best friends.

She just doesn't live in Stoneybrook anymore.

Dawn is tall, blonde, and blue-eyed, with an easygoing disposition and an intense love of all beach activities, including surfing. She doesn't eat red meat or sugar (she calls sugar "poison"!) and she is very environmentally conscious. She's also a great baby-sitter.

Not long after her mom and my dad got married, Dawn decided she missed California and her father too much to be able to make a new home in Stoneybrook after all. Her younger brother, Jeff, had made that decision earlier, and moved back to California. After much painful

MaryAnne

reflection, Dawn went to join him and her father and her father's new wife. So now Dawn is a West Coast baby-sitter. She belongs to a more laid-back baby-sitting group called the We ❤ Kids Club. Dawn and I stay in close touch, and she visits whenever she can. I miss her. We all do.

One baby-sitter who hasn't moved at all is Claudia Kishi. Claudia, who still lives in the same house on Bradford Court, is a talented artist and a junk food gourmet. In both capacities she has helped the BSC: by designing fliers, to distribute when we need business, as well as by making decorations for various BSC events, and by catering our BSC meetings with junk food from the supply she keeps hidden around her room. Her parents, not surprisingly, do not approve of Claudia's appreciation for such sugar-loaded snacks.

But then, they don't always understand Claudia. Claudia's older sister Janine is a genuine genius who is already taking college courses, because she's way past what they are teaching in her high school classes. Claudia, on the other hand, has so much trouble with schoolwork that someone in her family goes over her homework with her every night.

I personally believe that Claudia is a genius, too: the kind of genius who sees the world in a

26

way that doesn't always make sense to more ordinary people, such as school officials.

Claudia's creativity is evident in everything she does, from her spelling to the way she dresses. She has her own personal style, which, combined with her natural beauty, makes her the club knock-out. She makes most of her own jewelry, and creates amazing outfits from secondhand store finds, yard sales, whatever catches her eye. Her long dark hair, pale creamy skin, and dark brown eyes look perfect with everything she puts on.

Claudia's best friend is Stacey McGill, our treasurer. Stacey is as good at school as Claudia is bad at it. But when it comes to style, she and Claudia are on par. Like Claudia, Stace is tall with pale skin. But her hair is golden blond, her eyes are blue, and her style is New York sophisticated. For example, today, while Claudia was no doubt running around Stoneybrook in some tribute to the season that included Halloween colors and themes (last year it was Doc Martens with pumpkin stickers, a hand-batiked shirt in orange and black, plus one orange sock and one black sock), Stacey had gone for almost total black: black jeans, black boots, black turtleneck, silver cropped top over that, black boots with silver side buttons and silver X earrings. She looked stunning.

Mary Anne

Though she's Claudia's best friend, Stacey doesn't share Claudia's love of junk food. That's because she can't. Stacey has diabetes, which means that her body can't handle sugar properly. It also means no sweets for Stacey, ever, plus she has to give herself insulin shots every day. Stacey has tremendous self-control, though it hasn't always been that way. It took her awhile to realize that she had to take care of herself and stick to her special diet. Then she had to convince her parents, who are divorced now, that she could handle it all. Which she does, and which may explain why she often seems a little more mature than the rest of us.

The newest member of the club, who replaced Dawn as alternate officer, is Abigail Stevenson. Abby, her twin sister Anna, and their mother recently moved from Long Island to a house down the street from Kristy. Abby's father was killed in a car wreck a few years ago, something Abby never talks about. She'll talk about everything else, though. I mean, Abby will say *anything*. She even argues with Kristy. I think she actually enjoys it.

Despite that, Abby and Kristy get along pretty well. Abby even helps out as the assistant coach of Kristy's Krushers, a little kids' softball team that Kristy put together.

And while Kristy is a dedicated player and

rabid sports fan, Abby is what some people call a natural athlete. She's always in training. She doesn't walk anywhere if she can run. She's on the soccer team, and when it's not soccer season, she, like Logan, is on the lookout for any sport around. She's very competitive. I've heard her say that there is no such thing as second place.

Abby is also, as she puts it, "allergic to life." She dubbed her school bus the Wheeze Wagon because she said it sounded allergic like her. (Statements like that are typical of Abby's wild sense of humor. And she loves puns, the worse the better.) So, like Stacey, Abby has to watch what she eats. She also has to watch what she breathes: along with her allergies, she has asthma. Abby carries an inhaler with her at all times, in case she has an asthma attack. If she does, the inhaler helps her breathe. And if it doesn't work, she has to go to the hospital. That's happened to her once since she moved here, but it doesn't happen very often.

Abby has wild, curly brown hair and brown eyes, and wears contacts or glasses, depending on how she feels. She is a bit of a loner, but I don't think she is lonely. Abby is probably the most independent person I know, in part because her mother expects her and Anna to be able to take care of themselves, since she works very long hours and has a lengthy commute to her job in New York City.

Jessi Ramsey and Mallory Pike are our junior officers. They are junior officers because they are both eleven and in the sixth grade, and they aren't allowed to baby-sit at night except for their own families. They are also best friends, just like Claudia and Stacey, and Kristy and me.

Jessi is strong but lightly built. If that doesn't make sense, think of the ballet dancers you've seen — muscles of steel, but looking, just the same, as if they might leap into the sky and stay there. Jessi looks like a ballet dancer because she is one. She studies with a special teacher two afternoons a week *and* she gets up every morning at exactly 5:29 A.M. to practice at the barre in her basement. Her hard work has paid off. She has already had parts in real ballets, including *The Nutcracker.*

Like many ballerinas, Jessi often wears her hair pulled back in a bun. She has dark brown eyes and brown skin. Jessi's fond of wearing leotards even when she is not dancing; she has them in every color imaginable. She lives in an extended family. That means that in addition to her mother, father, younger sister, and younger brother, her aunt also lives with her.

Horses are another passion of Jessi's, and one

she shares with Mallory. They both love reading, especially horse stories (and mysteries).

But Mal will never be a ballet dancer. She is not crazy about anything athletic. Her plans are in another direction: writing. She wants to be a children's book author and illustrator when she grows up. She's already won an award for her writing and even had a temporary job helping out a famous children's writer who lives in Stoneybrook.

Like her seven siblings, Mallory has reddish-brown hair. She also has pale skin and freckles *and*, to her eternal despair, glasses and braces. And I don't need to add, I guess, that with seven younger brothers and sisters, she has had a ton of baby-sitting experience.

Logan, as I mentioned, is my boyfriend. He looks just like the star Cam Geary. At least I think he does, and *anybody* will tell you that he is very, very cute. He moved to Stoneybrook from Kentucky and has a nice southern drawl, blondish brown hair and kind blue eyes.

Shannon Kilbourne, our other associate member, maintains a full schedule at the private school she attends, which is why she is an associate member of the club — she'd never be able to fit regular meetings into afternoons crammed with French club, science club, homework (she's an outstanding student), and what sometimes sounds like a hundred other after-school activities. She's the only one of us who has to wear a school uniform. Claudia and Stacey, among others, consider this a hardship. The uniform, however, looks good on Shannon. Like Claudia and Stacey, she's one of those knockouts who could make anything look good. She has blond hair, blue eyes, and high cheekbones. And as you might expect of someone who excels at everything else she does, she excels at baby-sitting, too.

I couldn't help thinking, as I mentally reviewed the club members, that Kristy didn't have anything to worry about. The club was in great hands. I was just about to point this out to her when the bus slowed down and Mallory pressed her face against the window so fast her glasses clicked against the pane.

"Look!" she cried, fogging up the window. "There it is! The Salem Gables! And *look who is standing in front of it*. It's Martha Kempner!"

CHAPTER 4

Mallory ☺

Thursday

Halloween must be my lucky holiday. That's what I thought, anyway, as the bus pulled up to the door of the hotel and I saw who was standing there.

I could *not* believe my eyes, but it was true. I wanted to leap off the bus, run to her, and tell her how much I admired her — how I read her articles in newspapers and magazines every chance I got, and how I had read every single one of her mysteries. (I knew better than to ask her when she was going to write her next mystery, though. Writers hate questions like that.)

But first, of course, we had to listen to Ms. Garcia go over our instructions one more time, and then we had to wait for the driver to get our suitcases from the luggage compartment.

I thought I would die before I finally found mine. I grabbed the handle and dashed into the inn.

She was still there, standing to one side of the lobby, as if she were waiting for someone. Without giving myself time to think, I walked right up to her. I put down my suitcase, stuck out my right hand and said, "Uh, hi." Then I turned bright red, which looks particularly dumb when you have red hair. The thought of how stupid I looked made me blush even more.

But Ms. Kempner didn't seem to notice. She smiled and replied, "Hello," a note of inquiry in her voice.

I pulled myself together and plunged in. "Uh,

I'm Mallory Pike. That doesn't mean anything to you, of course. But I'm a fan of your work. You are the greatest writer. Really!"

Ms. Kempner shook my hand then and smiled again. "Thank you. Mallory, is it? I'm glad you like my writing."

"I love it," I said. "Totally, totally love it."

I realized, with a little shock, that although Ms. Kempner stood head and shoulders above most of the writers in the world in terms of her work, in person she was *short*. In fact, she was barely taller than me, an average-sized kid. And Ms. Kempner was wearing what looked like three-inch heels!

Dragging my gaze away from those painful-looking shoes, I heard myself say, to my horror, "Are you here to do research for a mystery?"

Of course, I turned red again.

Ms. Kempner didn't look offended. "My visit to Salem is in the nature of a working vacation, yes. But not for a mystery. I'm doing a piece on the Witch's Eye."

By now the rest of the kids were piling into the lobby, causing the noise level to rise. I could hear Mr. Blake repeating instructions, telling everybody to sign in at the desk, to make a line, and to please keep it quiet, this was an inn not a gymnasium.

I inched a little closer to Ms. Kempner, fascinated by her words. "The Witch's Eye?" I breathed.

"Yes. You don't know about the Witch's Eye? You will. It's on display at the Trove House Museum here in Salem, right at the end of the block. It's a large, nearly perfect yellow diamond, almost the size of a small egg. Yellow diamonds are not usually considered so valuable, but the color of this one is quite remarkable. And of course, any diamond of that size is going to be extraordinarily valuable."

"Why is it called the —"

"The Witch's Eye? Well, that's why I'm here. To try to separate fact from legend about it. The color, I imagine, has something to do with it. But it is also supposed to come with a horrible curse. It belongs to Mrs. Agatha Moorehouse, who's staying at the inn, too. In fact, there she is."

I turned and saw an older woman with silver frosted hair and deeply tanned skin, dressed in bright colors that somehow didn't go with the cross expression on her face. She was sitting in a wheelchair, frowning up at a younger, sturdy-looking Asian woman who was dressed in jeans and a sweater.

Ms. Kempner waved at them. Mrs. Moorehouse just looked sour, but the Asian woman waved back.

"We have an interview and lunch date," said

Ms. Kempner. "But if you are going to be here for awhile —"

"Four days," I croaked.

"Then I'm sure we'll meet again. In fact, I'll sign one of my books for you if you like."

Resolving to find a bookstore instantly and buy *all* of Ms. Kempner's books, I nodded. "That would be great," I managed to say.

I stood there in a daze, watching Ms. Kempner tap-tap-tap across the old, wide plank floors of the inn to Mrs. Moorehouse and her companion.

"Mallory! Hello?" It was Kristy, with Stacey, Abby, and Mary Anne right behind her. They swept me into the creaky old elevator and up to my room. Our rooms were all in a row. Abby and Stacey were in one room, Kristy and Mary Anne in the next, and then came mine. I had been assigned a room with another sixth-grader, Eileen Murphy.

I'd somehow forgotten about that, and I admit my heart sank when I opened the door and saw her there, carefully unpacking her suitcase. Then I thought, what do you know about Eileen, Mal? It's not as if you've ever really talked to her. She's probably perfectly nice, just a little shy. She's certainly not a witch.

I put my own suitcase on the bed. "I'm going to unpack later," I said.

"Is it okay that I took this bed?" asked Eileen nervously, staring at the wall above my head. "I mean, I can switch if you . . ."

"No, no, that's fine." Feeling virtuous, I said, "Hey, we're all going to go have dinner downstairs. You want to join us?"

What did I expect — that she would jump at the chance to be a part of our group? That she would be grateful?

Well, maybe I did. I don't know. I do know I was annoyed when Eileen bit her lip and shook her head.

"Fine," I said, a little shortly. "See you later then."

I met the others in the hall, and we went back down to the dining room.

"This is such a cool place," remarked Stacey as we seated ourselves at a big, round polished table. "I mean, look at it."

For the first time, I took a look at the inn.

We were in a long, narrow dining room full of tables like ours, and high-backed, upholstered chairs. On the papered walls were pictures of ships and a framed collection of knots used by sailors, neatly labeled. Old-fashioned lamps hung from the ceiling, and through tall windows framed by heavy curtains I could see the twinkling lights of Salem Commons. I had read about Salem Commons in one of the guidebooks. It had mentioned that our inn's dining room had a view of the Commons, where the militia used to drill.

"Mr. Blake and Coach Wu and Mrs. Bernhardt have posted their tour schedules for tomorrow," said Kristy briskly. "We can sign up for all kinds of tours: The House of the Seven Gables, which is what Nathaniel Hawthorne wrote his book about."

"He wrote *The Scarlet Letter*, too," I put in.

"But not the movie version," cracked Stacey. "Ugh."

"Okay, two gables down on the movie," Abby joked right back, holding up her hands and turning two thumbs down, the way the movie critics do.

After we'd made our crucial dinner-ordering decisions, Kristy focused her attention on me. "What about that famous author, Mallory? Did you land another job working for a writer?"

"I wish," I said. "Martha Kempner writes awesome mysteries."

"Salem's a great place for a mystery," suggested Stacey.

I shook my head. "That's what I thought too, but she's not here researching a mystery. Actually, it's something even more interesting than that. She's here to write an article on the Witch's Eye."

Kristy and Abby looked blank. Mary Anne frowned hard, as if she were trying to remember where she'd heard of it.

Stacey said, "Oh, yeah. I remember hearing about that on a class trip to the Museum of Natural History." She grinned suddenly. "When you are a kid in New York, you take *lots* of class trips to the museum. It's one of those famous jewels with a curse, right? But it's privately owned. I mean, it wasn't on display in the museum. They didn't even have a picture of it."

"It's on display now," I said triumphantly. "At the Trove House Museum on the corner."

"Isn't that your author, Ms. Kempner, now?" asked Kristy.

"Shh. Don't stare!" I hissed.

So of course we all did. Ms. Kempner had just come into the room, with Agatha Moorehouse. Her head was bent slightly as she talked. The same young woman was with them, pushing Mrs. Moorehouse's wheelchair.

"That's the woman who owns the Witch's Eye, Mrs. Moorehouse, in the wheelchair. I don't know who . . ."

"Naomi Furusawa," announced Kristy importantly. Seeing how surprised we were, she looked smug and a little sheepish. "I, uh, kind of overheard Mrs. Moorehouse introduce her to

Ms. Kempner in the lobby. Ms. Furusawa is Mrs. Moorehouse's nurse."

"What *is* the curse on the Witch's Eye?" I asked Stacey.

"I don't remember," Stacey said. "Something awful."

"Curses usually are," commented Abby, rolling her eyes.

At that moment our attention was distracted by the arrival of more SMS students. With Kristy in charge, we naturally had been the first ones to the dining room for dinner. I don't need to add that Kristy was very pleased with herself, not only for being first, but for securing a table in the corner of the room where we could watch everybody. Of course that suited me fine, because I wanted to watch Martha (okay, so she hadn't said I could call her Martha, but I did in my mind, since I was a future fellow writer).

"Jerk alert," said Abby loudly as Alan steered toward our table.

Alan was completely oblivious to the hostile silence that met his cheerful greeting. "Hey," he said. "I just wanted to say I'm sorry about the spaghetti. No hard feelings, okay?"

"Go *away*, Alan," said Kristy. Alan put his hand over his heart, pretended to look hurt, and staggered away to his table, where Cary and some other guys were sitting. They all seemed to think this was really funny.

I thought something else was funny. Funny peculiar. I caught Stacey's sleeve. "Look at that guy," I hissed. "The one in the corner, in the navy blue sweater."

Stacey glanced in the direction I'd indicated. "Boring," she said. "Not date material for any age group."

"That's not what I'm talking about," I said. "I'm talking about the way he's reading that newspaper he brought in with him. He keeps looking around the edge of it toward Martha, I mean, Ms. Kempner's table. And he hasn't turned a single page."

"He's a slow reader. Easily distracted. Too much MTV," suggested Stacey.

"I'm serious!"

"You're letting this Witch City business affect you, Mal. Just because we're in a historic inn and there is a famous mystery writer here."

"And the owner of a *cursed* diamond, don't forget."

"Whatever," Stacey said. "Still, it doesn't mean that everyone is a suspicious character. Besides, as a spy, his look just doesn't work, if you know what I mean."

"What are you talking about, Stacey?" asked Kristy.

42

Mallory
ะ์

"Well, the suit is okay. Boring, which is a good thing in a spy, because you don't want to be noticed. But the sneakers? Puh-lease! That look is so fifteen years ago in New York. Trust me. It's the spooky atmosphere of this inn that is making you —"

"Spooky?" Mary Anne's attention had been caught by that one word. "Spooky? You think this inn is spooky?"

"Sure," said Stacey.

"Haunted, I bet," Kristy put in. "Listen for footsteps in the corridors. Doors closing. Moans from the closet."

"And the sound of marching footsteps from the Commons," I added, "where ghostly militiamen still drill."

Mary Anne's eyes widened. She looked over her shoulder. Then she took a deep breath and said, "Well, I live in a haunted house. What are a few more ghosts?"

Abby let out a hoot. "Good for you, Mary Anne!"

Just then our dinners came, and we settled down to business.

Suddenly, Kristy looked up, scowling ferociously.

"What is it, Kristy?" asked Mary Anne. Then she held up a hand. "No gross food jokes. This *isn't* the school cafeteria."

"Yeah, this stuff's actually good," put in Abby.

Without answering, Kristy twisted around and looked down. Then she jumped up, reached into her chair, and produced a small, very melted-looking piece of ice.

"My chair is wet. And my pants and my shirt!" exclaimed Kristy. "How did that happen?"

Another burst of laughter from Alan's table answered that question. Kristy whirled, and I thought for a moment she was going to bean Alan with the rest of the ice cube. Abby caught her arm just in time.

"Hey. You want to land in trouble for starting a food fight or something?" asked Abby. "And you know you'll be the one they blame."

"But — but — but —" sputtered Kristy. Steam was practically coming out of her ears.

"Sit down, Kristy," said Mary Anne. She reached out and plucked a napkin from another table. "Here, you can put this over your seat."

Kristy sat down. "Alan Gray isn't really in eighth grade. His true mental age is three and a half."

"You'll get him back, Kristy," said Abby. She grinned. "But wait until you're not so angry and can think clearly. Remember, 'Revenge is a dish best served cold.'"

44

We all stared at her. Abby raised her eyebrows in mock surprise. "You never heard that?"

We ate dinner peacefully for awhile, a few vengeful grumblings and glares in Alan's direction by Kristy aside. I kept an eye on the newspaper spy (as I had mentally dubbed the man I was still half-convinced was watching Martha's table). As I watched, another man, dressed like a banker or a lawyer, rose from his seat at a small table by the fireplace and walked across the room to Martha's table.

At about the same time, a large table full of noisy kids (plus two exhausted adults) got up and left. In the relative silence that followed, we could hear snatches of the conversation.

". . . Harvey Hapgood, and I must say, I'm delighted to meet you."

I saw an automatic smile form on Martha's face, and she opened her mouth to say something. Then she seemed to realize, as did I, that the man wasn't talking to her at all.

I gave Stacey a nudge. "Listen," I hissed.

All five of us immediately became unnaturally silent.

Mrs. Moorehouse allowed Harvey Hapgood to take her hand and make a sort of bow over it. He bent forward and lowered his voice, and we couldn't hear anything but the murmur of their

45

voices for a moment. Then Mrs. Moorehouse threw back her shoulders and lifted her chin. Her voice rang out: "Sell the Witch's Eye? Absolutely not. Good evening, Mr. Hapgood." Mrs. Moorehouse swiveled away from Mr. Hapgood, clearly ending the conversation.

He stood there for a moment, looking a little embarrassed. Then he turned away and went back to his table. Martha watched him go, drawing her eyebrows together. Then she, too, turned back to her table.

Just then, the waitress reappeared, to see if we wanted dessert. Having haunted houses and ghostly inns on our minds, we pumped her for information.

"Haunted? Salem Gables? Well, like any old house, it creaks and moans." The waitress shook her head. "The inn has always been an inn, and I'm sure it has had a lot of fascinating things happen in it. But nothing that produced any ghosts, as far as I know."

"No murders? No hidden treasure? No pirates ever slept here?"

Smiling, the waitress answered, "Pirates probably did. But most of them would have stayed in less expensive boarding houses meant for sailors and seafarers."

"Is it called Salem Gables after the House of the Seven Gables?" I asked.

"Yup. When the current owners bought it — oh, ten years or so ago — and fixed it up to make it a first-class inn again, they wanted to use the word 'witch' in the name. But they decided against it. Afraid it would put people off. Some people are as crazy about the idea of witches now as they were back in sixteen ninety-two."

As we left, a little while later, I couldn't help glancing over at the table where Martha Kempner sat. I noticed that she had brought out a small tape recorder and put it on the table. Almost totally ignoring her food, she was leaning forward eagerly, talking to Mrs. Moorehouse and occasionally to Ms. Furusawa. Her legs were crossed and I could see one high-heeled foot swinging back and forth at the edge of the tablecloth. I tried to catch Martha's eye, but her attention remained focused on Mrs. Moorehouse.

And the newspaper spy remained focused on Martha. Maybe he was a reporter doing a story about her, I thought. Or an unauthorized biography. But I didn't think so.

I really didn't believe he was just sitting there reading the newspaper, minding his own business, either. As far as I could tell, he still hadn't turned a single page. Not even my brothers linger over the sports section of the newspaper that long.

Mallory

For a moment, I almost wished I had brought along our mystery notebook, so I could jot down a description of the newspaper spy. Then I realized that we didn't have a mystery. Just my suspicions. Nothing had happened.

So I didn't need the notebook at all.

We spent the rest of the evening piled into Mary Anne and Kristy's room, which had high ceilings, a gabled window, and twin beds with flowered bedspreads that matched the curtains.

I couldn't resist bringing up the newspaper spy again. But everyone thought my theory that he might be an unauthorized biographer of Martha Kempner was totally lame. I had to agree. In fact, it sounded even more improbable when I said it aloud.

"So maybe it isn't Ms. Kempner he's watching," said Kristy. "Maybe it's Mrs. Moorehouse."

"Yeah. Yeah!" I liked the sound of that better. "To steal the diamond! That's it!"

The math-minded and ever-logical Stacey said, "Come on, if he were going to steal the diamond, he'd be casing the museum, not Mrs. Moorehouse."

"Boo-hoo, Cassandra Clue," said Abby, referring to a mystery show some of our clients had created and staged when they'd had to endure a ban on television.

The phone shrilled. Kristy picked it up and listened. Her eyes widened. She held the receiver away from her ear, and the rest of us could hear, faintly, a high pitched, "Boooooooo, boooooooo."

"Alan," decided Abby.

"Infantile brat!" Kristy snapped into the phone receiver, and slammed it down so hard, it made *my* ear hurt. I hoped it had made Alan's hurt, too.

"He's clearly having a second childhood," growled Kristy. "Not that he ever outgrew his first one." She folded her arms. "But one of these days, I'll have the last word with Alan Gray!"

CHAPTER 5

Stacey

Friday

Quiet. Beautiful. Peaceful. These are the words that came to mind when I looked out of our window at Salem Commons this morning. Was I ever wrong!

If the Salem Gables were haunted, the ghosts were very quiet ones. I slept straight through the night and woke to find a brisk, clear day in Salem. Through my window, which didn't have a gable like the one in Kristy's and Mary Anne's room, I could see joggers crossing Salem Commons, dogs playing in the center of it while their owners watched, a sign that said, "No dogs off leash," and a few early tourists already snapping pictures.

After everyone had eaten breakfast we assembled in the lobby to head off to the various events we'd signed up for. I was surprised that Mal wasn't going with Mary Anne and me on the museum tour, which was scheduled to stop at the Trove House Museum first. I thought she'd be dying to see the Witch's Eye. But when I found out she was going to go with Mrs. Bernhardt and a guide to visit the House of the Seven Gables, I understood why. (Kristy had signed up for that, too.)

A third group was going directly to the Salem Witch Museum, with Ms. Garcia. I saw with a sinking heart that Eileen had signed up for that. She was wearing a huge purple dress, a puffy orange windbreaker, and these really clunky shoes. Her hair stuck out in spikes beneath a wool hat that had a pattern of white snowflakes on a red background. She was fashion-challenged. But that wasn't really what made my heart sink. Everyone has bad fashion days. No, what worried me was the fact that Cokie and company had also signed up for the Witch Museum, and they were already subjecting Eileen to cruel jokes and teasing.

"Going to visit your great-grandmother, Eileen?" asked Cokie.

"I hear a dog was hanged a witch," said Grace. "Maybe that was Eileen's grandmother."

"Poor dog," said Eileen very, very softly.

Poor Eileen, I thought. Fortunately, Ms. Garcia showed up at that moment. After one look at the situation, she moved Cokie and Grace to the front of the group and assigned Eileen a partner at the back. (Yes, we were still on the buddy system, just like little kids on first-grade field trips.)

Abby was taking a different tour of Salem, along with Coach Wu and a couple of other kids who are into sports and athletics. Coach Wu explained, "There's a red line drawn on the sidewalks through Salem. If you follow that, it'll take you past most of the key historic places. I've done my homework, so I'll be able to tell you about them while we jog. We'll make a slight detour over to Chestnut Street, which isn't on the red line tour. It's a registered national landmark and has been called 'the finest, most aristocratic and best-preserved thoroughfare in North America.'"

I saw Abby grin and I knew she was thinking what I was thinking: You can take the teacher out of the school, but you can't take the teacher out of the teacher!

Our group was the first to set off.

Trove House Museum, just down the block from our inn, was one of several historic buildings that were surrounded by a big wall. One ticket allowed you to go in through the main gate and tour any of the houses.

Everybody else peeled off to other houses, but Mary Anne and I made a beeline for Trove House, which had just opened. We were the first in line. But we didn't see the Witch's Eye. We had barely made it up the stairs when an alarm went off.

In an instant, everything went from museum quiet to utter chaos. A guard charged past us, going in one direction. Then two more hurtled by going in the other, trailed by an agitated man and an agitated woman, both wearing suits. I recognized the agitated man as the one who had punched our tickets when we came through the door.

"What —" Mary Anne began to whisper. But

just then the woman zoomed by again, punching out numbers on a cellular phone and crying, "Lock the door! Lock the door!"

We flattened ourselves against the wall. Then Mary Anne said, "Are we going to be locked in here? I'm going to go find out."

"Mary Anne, wait." But before I could tell her I didn't think it was such a good idea, she had broken the cardinal rule of the buddy system, and we were separated.

I broke rule number two. I didn't wait in the place where we were separated so we could be reunited. I did what any normally curious person would do. I walked down the hall, toward the place where all the noise was coming from.

It was a big room, lined with low glass cases beneath soft track lights. Three more glass cases stood in the center of the room, each with an individual spotlight on it. A group had gathered around the glass case in the center and as I watched, two police officers hurried to join them, along with the woman holding the cellular phone.

Making myself as inconspicuous as possible, I edged around the door and leaned against the wall.

"No, I *know* I set the alarm," the agitated man insisted.

The woman nodded. "Naturally, I double-

checked it. And there is an automatic activation
system at any rate. It goes on by timer, but can
only be shut off manually by someone with a
key and the code. I turned off the alarm just a
few minutes ago."

A man in a guard's uniform said, "And I had
just walked into the room to begin guard duty
when I noticed the Witch's Eye was missing.
That's when I triggered the alarm manually."

"No overt sign of tampering with the case,"
said one police officer, whipping out her notebook and making a note.

"But who? And how? And when? Who could
have taken the Witch's Eye?" moaned the
woman.

"We're ruined," said the man.

The Witch's Eye! The Witch's Eye had been
stolen. I drew in a long breath. Was this the curse
of the Witch's Eye at work? I remembered the
"newspaper spy" that Mallory had been watching so suspiciously, and how I had dismissed
the idea that he was a thief. Had I been wrong?

Just then a scrap of white paper, half hidden
under the edge of the case next to me, caught my
eye. I bent down to pick it up. It was part of a
sheet of Salem Gables stationery, with a series of
numbers on it, printed in black ink. Of course,
they immediately imprinted themselves on my
brain, too. Numbers have a way of doing that.

For example, I was now stuck, at least for awhile, with the license plate of the bus on which we'd traveled to Salem.

My movement caught the attention of one of the guards. "Hey!" he exclaimed. "What are *you* doing in here?"

I looked up from the scrap of paper to find everyone who had gathered around the now-empty display case staring at me.

Don't act guilty, I told myself. Of course the fact that they were all staring at me as if I were a suspect didn't help.

"I'm here on a class trip," I squeaked out. "I had just come into the museum when the alarm went off."

The man in the suit suddenly nodded. "I remember you. You were here with a friend. Where is she?"

"We were separated in all the excitement," I said. It seemed the simplest explanation.

One of the police officers said sharply, "What's that in your hand?"

I'd almost forgotten about the piece of paper. "Oh. A piece of paper — stationery — with numbers on it. I just found it under this case right here." I walked forward, holding out the scrap of paper.

The officer took the piece of paper by its edge

and held it up. She read off the series of numbers. "This mean anything to anybody?"

Everyone shook their heads. Then the guard volunteered, "But this room is vacuumed and mopped every single night. That paper had to have landed on the floor since then."

The other officer produced a plastic lock-top bag and dropped the scrap of paper in it.

"Is it a clue?" I asked.

"You shouldn't be here," said the woman suddenly. "Unless the police want you for questioning?" She looked at the officers.

The first officer answered her. "I think we should secure the scene." Then she turned to me. "Give me your name and number and we'll contact you later if need be."

The officer, who was wearing a badge with the name Saxon on it, led me out of the room and wrote down my name, the name of the inn, the names of all of our chaperons, and my home address and phone number. "Thanks," she said. "You may go now." She nodded toward the stairs leading down to the museum entrance.

"You're welcome," I replied, trying to sound icily dignified, and miffed at being dismissed like a little kid. Adults! I was surprised she didn't say "Run along and play!"

I turned to go and my mouth dropped open.

Stacey

Mal's newspaper spy was bounding noiselessly up the steps. He reached the top, and passed by without even noticing me. I watched him, waiting for Officer Saxon to hold out her arm and order him to halt in the name of the law.

But she didn't. Instead, she leaned forward as the man held up what looked like a little wallet and flipped it open.

"Officer Saxon," said the man. "I'd like a complete briefing."

She nodded. "This way," she said.

And she led him inside.

CHAPTER 6

Mary Anne

Friday

I couldn't believe something like this was happening to us. And the robbery in the museum was just the beginning. Walking home to the inn, things became even more interesting.

Mary Anne

When I left Stacey, I headed straight for the front desk, where we'd had our tickets punched to admit us to Trove House. A guard appeared out of nowhere. "What are you doing here?" he practically screeched. "The museum is *closed.*"

I held up my ticket. "We just came in and —"

He didn't let me finish. "Well, you can just go back out." He put his hand on my shoulder and propelled me toward the door.

"But my friend is still —"

The guard's walkie-talkie crackled.

"Out, out, out," said the guard. He opened the front door of the museum and pushed me through. I heard it close with a final thunk behind me, and I was standing alone on the steps of the museum.

A small group of people had gathered on the walkway. They were watching a police car that had just pulled up at the entrance gate. Then they turned to look at me. I felt my face turn red. I didn't like having all those strangers staring at me. I walked down the stairs just as another guard appeared and began to herd the whole group of people toward the gate. They must have closed off the museum grounds, too, I realized. *What* was going on inside of Trove House? Where was Stacey? And where was the rest of my group?

The guard made us line up, and then he began to write down our names and addresses, checking identification for those who were old enough to have drivers' licenses. I learned the answer to my question about the rest of the group when it was my turn to sign out: the names of everybody else, except Stacey, were already on the list. The guard looked up when I said my name aloud, ran his finger down to where Mr. Blake's name was and said, "You're with the Stoneybrook school group, right? Your teacher said for you to go straight back to the inn."

I nodded. For a moment I considered loitering around the entrance to wait for Stacey. Then I realized that it would be pointless. When she checked out, the guard would tell her the same thing.

I headed back toward the inn, and turned down the path that led across the spacious lawn to the porch steps. Just as I put my foot on the bottom stair, I heard voices coming around the side of the inn. Something made me duck back into the evergreen bushes that grew beside the steps.

A moment later, I felt foolish when I realized that the voices belonged to Agnes Moorehouse and Naomi Furusawa. The nurse was wheeling Mrs. Moorehouse around from the other end of the porch, where there was a ramp.

Mary Anne

"I'm ruined! My fortune is gone! It's all over. I'll end up in the streets!" Mrs. Moorehouse intoned.

"You know that's not true," said Ms. Furusawa calmly. "Mrs. Moorehouse, you have plenty of money."

"Ha. That's what everyone thinks," said Mrs. Moorehouse sourly. "But the theft of that diamond will be the end of me, you mark my words."

"Now Mrs. Moorehouse —"

"Bankruptcy! Ruin! Or worse," cried Mrs. Moorehouse. "Ruined! Ruined! Faster, Naomi. Get me to that museum!" Mrs. Moorehouse thumped the arm of her wheelchair impatiently. I could see her clearly from my hiding place. Rings flashed on her fingers. Bracelets shone on her arms. There were more sparkles at her ears. I realized that her hands had sparkled in much the same way the night before, as had her earlobes and her wrists. The Witch's Eye wasn't the only jewel Mrs. Moorehouse owned, unless all those rings and earrings and bracelets were fakes.

The nurse, her expression surprisingly patient and untroubled, pushed Mrs. Moorehouse quickly down the path. She was as plainly dressed as Mrs. Moorehouse was dressed up. Although she wasn't wearing a uniform, her outfit was almost exactly the same as the day before: pants, a cotton sweater, a blouse, comfortable shoes.

She wasn't very big, I noted, but she seemed strong. At Mrs. Moorehouse's command, Ms. Furusawa had quickened her pace easily. A moment later the wheelchair bumped onto the sidewalk and disappeared from sight in the direction of the museum.

The diamond? Stolen? Did she mean the Witch's Eye? My heart skipped a beat. Was that what the alarm was all about? I stared after Mrs. Moorehouse. If the diamond had been stolen, someone must have just called her and told her about it, I reasoned. There was no other way she could have known about it so fast.

But why was she saying she would be bankrupt? To own a famous gem like the Witch's Eye, Mrs. Moorehouse had to be a wealthy woman. And I wasn't sure, but I didn't think people hired nurses to wheel them around unless they could afford to pay out a good amount of money. Then again, maybe insurance paid for that.

Wait. Insurance! Surely Mrs. Moorehouse had insured the diamond. So even if the Witch's Eye were the most valuable thing she owned, and it was stolen, wouldn't she get an enormous amount of insurance on it?

Mary Anne

I mean, you couldn't own something like the Witch's Eye without having it insured. Then I remembered my father reminding Sharon, my stepmother, to pay the car insurance or she'd be driving without any insurance at all.

Had Mrs. Moorehouse forgotten to pay her insurance? Could that be why she was so upset?

Where was Stacey? The questions were churning in my brain, and since she'd managed to stay in the museum longer than I had, I was sure she would have some more information.

Besides, Stacey would know about things like insurance. At least, I hoped she would. People who are good at math usually know things like that.

I suddenly realized that I was still crouched in the bushes. Good grief! What if someone came along and found me there? How would I explain that?

I put my hand down to push myself upright. It touched something soft and furry and very, very dead.

I began to scream.

CHAPTER 7

Abby

Friday

A nice educational jog through the streets of a town is not a bad way to learn the layout of a place. Salem is a very pleasant town to jog through, and it was fun to have a built-in tour guide in Coach Wu. Then I felt an all-too-familiar feeling....

Abby

A blister! Just what I needed! That's what happens when you don't stick to your tried and true brand of socks, I thought sourly.

Not that it was a blister yet. Just one of those rubbed sore spots that could become a blister.

I decided not to take any chances. I pulled alongside Coach Wu and told her the problem. With her permission, I peeled off from the jogging group as we swung back past the inn on our way toward the wharf.

"Don't go anywhere else unless you clear it with another chaperon first," she reminded me.

"Right," I said. Where did she think I was going to go with a potential blister on my foot? Right up to my room to put gel and a Band-Aid on it, that's where.

But first, I nearly went to the moon. Really.

I'd just reached the porch when a blood-curdling scream erupted from the bushes by the side steps. I leaped in the air and let out a little scream of my own, one of pure surprise. My heart stopped, I swear.

As I returned to earth, cutting my own vocals short, I recognized the screamer.

"Mary Anne!" I cried, and made a mad dash toward the sound. I hurtled down the steps and spun to face the bushes, which were swaying wildly.

"Help me! Get it off me!" Mary Anne was nearly in tears.

I stopped, and my heartbeat returned to something like normal. I stared, and then I couldn't help it. I started to laugh.

Mary Anne was engaged in hand-to-hand combat with what appeared to be a large black wig. I didn't blame her for screaming. If I had a wig like that attack me, I'd have screamed, too.

"Mary Anne. It's okay!" I said. Reaching into the bushes, I tore the wig from her hand. I held it up and shook it. "See?"

"Abby!" gasped Mary Anne. She emerged from the bushes, her face red. She was panting.

"Having a bad hair day?" I asked sympathetically. "Or did you scalp somebody?"

Mary Anne looked from my face to my hand. "Oh," she said.

"If you don't mind my asking, what are you doing lurking in the bushes? And where is everybody else?"

"Uh, they've already come back from the museum. We had to leave early. There was a robbery."

"You're kidding!"

"No! The Witch's Eye was stolen from the

Trove Museum. They discovered it just as Stacey and I walked in. Then she and I were separated."

"And you were looking for Stacey in the bushes?"

"No," said Mary Anne seriously. "I hid because . . . well, I don't know why. I heard someone coming and I just sort of ducked."

"Looks like you aren't the first."

We both studied the wig. It was made of long, straight, shiny black hair. Up close, it didn't look very natural. How had a wig ended up in the bushes? I looked up, vaguely wondering if it could have fallen out of a window.

Mary Anne looked down at the ground and said, "There's something else, something shiny."

"Maybe it's the Witch's Eye," I suggested. I was kidding.

Mary Anne didn't seem to notice. "No," she answered soberly. She bent forward and pushed her way back into the bushes. "It's sunglasses," she said. "I guess the sunlight was reflecting off the lenses. And look at this!"

"What? *What?*" I couldn't see past the branches, or Mary Anne, who was squatting on the ground now.

"Clothes," she said.

"Kids playing games," I suggested. "Like Alan Gray?"

"I don't think so." Mary Anne backed out and turned around, holding out the sunglasses and what looked like a custodian's jumpsuit. The name of the museum was embroidered in fancy script on the pocket.

"Why would a custodian hide his — or her — stuff in the bushes here?" I said slowly.

"The robbery!" gasped Mary Anne. "Maybe that's how the thief got into the museum unnoticed."

I'd been reaching out for the sunglasses, but I drew my hand back. If they were a clue, the fewer fingerprints on them the better, although of course the criminal had probably used gloves. All criminals used gloves, didn't they? It was standard criminal procedure.

"The robbery," I repeated. "Uh-oh." I had a bad feeling suddenly. A mystery-is-about-to-happen feeling. Why had I thought for an instant that we'd have a nice, peaceful trip to Salem?

"Tell me about the robbery," I said, taking Mary Anne by the arm and steering her up the stairs. "Tell me all about it while we find someone who can take charge of this stuff. And call the police."

One of the owners of the inn, Mr. Hewson, was at the front desk. He sprang into action immediately and wouldn't even let me go upstairs

Abby

to fix my potential blister before the police arrived.

I was walking — with an exaggerated limp — toward the gift shop just as Mr. Hewson, who was still on the phone with the police, said, "Martha Kempner? Yes. She just walked into the gift shop. Yes, I'll tell her."

He hung up the phone and called out, "Ms. Kempner!" When she didn't respond, he turned to us. "Girls — Mary Anne, Abby — would you please tell Ms. Kempner I need to give her a message?"

"Yes, we'll be glad to," said Mary Anne politely.

I kept limping. When I reached the door of the gift shop, which was at an angle from the front desk, I said, "Ms. Kempner? You're wanted at the check-in desk."

Martha Kempner turned, a surprised expression on her face. She was even shorter than I remembered her to be. "Me?" she said.

"Yes," I said. "Mr. Hewson asked us to tell you."

"Oh. Well. Thank you." Ms. Kempner bounded out.

That's when I saw the pumpkin. It was in a basket of hokey souvenirs near the door, a one-of-a-kind item calling my name. (I love souvenirs. You should see what I brought back

70

from Hawaii!) I scooped it up. It was made of that fake ceramic stuff that doesn't break easily, and painted a really bright orange. It had round eyes and a toothy grin. For a moment I thought it was part of a salt-and-pepper-shaker set that had lost its mate. But it wasn't the right size and lacked the holes in the head.

"The perfect pet," I announced to the gift shop at large. "You don't have to walk it, house train it, clean its litter, or take it to the vet. And, more importantly, I couldn't possibly be allergic to it." When I couldn't find a price tag, I took the pumpkin over to the gift shop counter. "How much?"

The shop clerk was leaning over the far end of the counter, staring out at the lobby, wide-eyed. The police had arrived. One officer was talking to Mr. Hewson. I didn't see any others or Ms. Kempner, so I assumed she was being interviewed separately. Mary Anne was perched on a chair, looking apprehensive.

"How much?" I repeated, as the clerk turned her head reluctantly toward me.

"What? Oh." She stared at the pumpkin I was balancing on my palm and wrinkled her forehead. "Gosh, I don't know. Isn't there a price on it?"

Would I have asked if there had been a price on it? No. "No," I said aloud.

71

"Where did you find it?"

"Over there," I said, pointing to the basket.

"Oh. I thought I knew all the merchandise, but that's a new one. There must have been a new shipment, and the boss put stuff out without telling me."

"So how much?" I asked for the third time. I was feeling a little impatient. My foot hurt, I hadn't finished my run, and I was about to be grilled by the police. I mean, give me a break.

"I don't know."

"I'll give you two bucks," I said. "It's got a little crack here at the bottom, see?"

The clerk thought for a moment, then shrugged. "Deal," she agreed. Pleased with my bargain, I paid for the pumpkin and carried it out into the lobby.

Mary Anne was now in conversation with one of the police officers. She turned, saw me, and said, "There she is. Abby Stevenson. She was with me when we found the jumpsuit and the glasses."

"And I helped her subdue the wig," I couldn't resist saying.

The inspector, a short, plump man with sideburns that made his round face seem even rounder, was not a jolly man. He did not smile. He wrote something in his notebook and said,

"Abby Stevenson. And you and Mary Anne Spier are friends from school?"

I started to say that I had never seen the girl before in my life. But my instinct for self-preservation stopped me. I nodded.

The inspector (whose name was Frizell) motioned for us to sit down. Mary Anne and I pulled up a pair of antique chairs. Officer Frizell lowered himself onto a little bench and asked us lots and lots of questions. It was like taking a really boring test. At least I know all the answers, I thought.

"Thank you," Detective Frizell said at last. "I believe I have all I need here."

"You're welcome," said Mary Anne the ever-polite.

"Our pleasure," I added.

Frizell pocketed his notebook and walked away.

Mary Anne and I locked eyes. We didn't have to say it. Each knew what the other was thinking.

A mystery had fallen into our laps. This was a job for the Baby-sitters Club.

CHAPTER 8

Jessi

Friday

So far, Jordan hasn't turned anybody into a toad. Or a sofa cushion or a cat or anything. But when I arrived at Mal's house to baby-sit with Shannon, all the Halloween chaos spelled trouble!

"**E**ye of bat and apple core, beware who enters by that door!" chanted Jordan dramatically as Shannon and I walked into the Pike den. Sometimes we only need one sitter at the Pikes', if the triplets are around. But today, Mrs. Pike requested two. It wasn't hard to see why.

"I can fly, I can fly, I can fly," shrieked five-year-old Claire, racing through the room. A pair of large cardboard wings was attached to her back. They were crooked. If she had managed to fly, she would not have flown in a straight line. But then what little kid ever even *runs* in a straight line?

"I'll catch you yet, with my net," sang her older sister Vanessa. Vanessa wasn't casting a spell. She wants to be a poet and frequently speaks in rhyme. She zipped through the room after Claire, a large net held high. Vanessa rarely moves that fast; she's more often found writing poetry in one of her "private" notebooks.

I ducked one way and Shannon ducked another as they burst out of the room.

"See," said Jordan, "I told you to beware." Then he ran out, too.

Mrs. Pike stuck her head in the door. "You just need to keep the insanity to a medium level until five-thirty," she told Shannon and me.

Jessi

"I'm hoping they'll burn off some Halloween energy early."

"No problem," I said. Secretly, I was wondering whether Shannon and I wouldn't need a book of baby-sitting spells. Not that either of us believe for one minute in spells. There is no such thing as a spell.

But clearly the Pikes were either believing, or pretending they believed, in Jordan's newly acquired spell-casting abilities, and I couldn't help thinking that maybe baby-sitters could play this game, too, turning it to our advantage. Not that we necessarily needed drastic measures of any sort with the Pikes. They represent high energy compounded by sheer numbers, but baby-sitting for them is usually fun, not like sitting for sullen or rude kids. Or those kids — like this family we once sat for — whose parents were serious bigots, and were trying to teach their kids to behave the same way. If spells really worked, they would have been good candidates.

Come to think of it, if those people had been moved back in time a few hundred years, I could imagine them accusing other people of being witches and wanting them hanged for it.

Hmmm.

"I hate to ask, 'Where is everybody,' but . . ." Shannon said to me as soon as Mrs. Pike had gone. She and I were now standing in an empty den. Pike-free.

I was still thinking about spells. I said, "Maybe Jordan put a spell on the whole family and made them invisible."

"Shh! Don't give him any ideas," said Shannon in mock horror.

She and I split up and went to hunt for the various Pikes.

Nicky, who's eight, was in his room, with coins spread out around him. He looked up when Shannon poked her head into his room and said, "Hi."

"You look like a banker," Shannon teased him. "Is that how we're going to be paid for baby-sitting today? In pennies?"

Nicky peered at her through his glasses, then smiled slightly. "No. Dad brought home rolls of pennies from the bank and I'm going through them to find old ones that are valuable. You can do that sometimes. I once found an old penny that was worth five whole dollars!"

"That's a good return on the investment," Shannon commented.

"Uh-huh," said Nicky, losing interest in Shannon and the conversation as he opened another roll of pennies and spread it out on the floor around him.

Vanessa and Claire had abandoned their chase

and had also taken to the floor. They were in Vanessa's room, with Claire's cardboard wings spread out flat, along with what looked like at least a hundred crayons, plus the "B" volume of the *World Book Encyclopedia*, open to the color plates of butterflies. Margo, who is seven, was with them, too.

Shannon didn't need to ask what was going on. Clearly, the wings were about to be decorated butterfly-style.

Meanwhile, I had tracked Jordan, Byron, and Adam down to the dining room table. Make that *under* the dining room table. They were huddled beneath it with a blanket draped over the top. The lights were off and Jordan was holding a flashlight to illuminate the blanket cave.

As I lifted up one side of the blanket, Jordan whisked something out of sight. "Halt," he said, making his voice deep. "Who goes there? Who dares enter Merlin's Cave?"

"Hi, guys. What's up?"

The triplets exchanged glances. Then Jordan intoned, "We shake, we bake, our spells to make."

"What have you got there? The Shake 'n Bake Spell book?" I couldn't resist asking.

"Be gone or be poofed!" said Jordan thunderously.

78

Jessi

"Poofed?" I asked. I didn't laugh. And it wasn't easy.

"Poofed. You know, I cast a spell on you and 'poof!' you vanish. Or turn into something else," said Jordan.

Adam and Byron nodded solemnly. Then Adam added, "We're working on a spell to help Claire fly when she is wearing her butterfly wings."

Holding up my hands and letting the edge of the blanket drop, I said, "I'm poofing, I'm poofing." I headed toward the den and met Shannon on her way back from Vanessa's room. For the moment, at least, the Pikes were all relatively peacefully occupied. But that could change at any second. Like good baby-sitters, Shannon and I decided to be prepared by having a snack ready and waiting in the kitchen. We also decided that in half an hour, even if there hadn't been any eruptions, we'd gather everyone together to eat the snack.

"And maybe we should just mention that you can't *really* cast spells, and you shouldn't believe in them," I suggested. I told Shannon about the flying magic the triplets were concocting for Claire.

"Yes," agreed Shannon. "Although Claire will probably find out soon enough, if she tries to fly."

79

Jessi

At that moment the phone rang.

I picked it up. "Pike residence," I said.

"Jessi? It's me. Mal."

"Mallory! Hey! Are you guys having fun?"

"I can't fill you in right now, Jessi. I don't have time. This is important!" said Mal urgently.

I snapped to attention. "Mal, what is it? What's wrong?"

Shannon, who had been putting out plates and napkins, looked up.

"The Witch's Eye has been stolen. Stacey and Mary Anne were in the museum when the alarm went off. Kristy and I were at the House of the Seven Gables, but Stacey found a clue in the museum and then Mary Anne and Abby found another one in the bushes outside the hotel. . . ."

I looked at the phone. Had Jordan cast a long-distance spell on Mallory, making her lose her reason? "Mal! Mallory! Slow down. You're not making any sense. For starters, what *is* a Witch's Eye?"

I could hear Mallory take a deep breath at the other end of the phone. "Sorry," she said at last. "There is this diamond —"

"Wait a minute. I think Shannon should hear this, too." Shannon nodded and whisked out of the kitchen. A minute later I heard the click of the extension in the den being picked up.

"Hi, Mallory," said Shannon. "What's up?"

Mallory took another deep breath. "There is a famous diamond called the Witch's Eye," she began. "And it is right here in Salem, on display for Halloween. Or it was, until it was stolen from the Trove House Museum this morning."

We listened closely as Mallory told us what had happened. When she'd finished, Shannon said, "Amazing. Absolutely amazing. You went on a perfectly ordinary school trip and you've landed in the middle of a mystery."

"Yes," said Mallory, "but I can't solve it without your help."

I admit it. As Mal was talking, I *had* been feeling a little envious and left out of the adventure. Now this was more like it! I immediately started feeling better. "Definitely!" I said. "What do you want us to do? Research at the library? Follow a local suspect? You name it."

We baby-sitters have done all that and more, in the process of solving other mysteries.

But Mal's next words punctured that balloon. "No, no, no," she said impatiently. "Nothing like that. Just send me the mystery notebook. I — we — *have* to have it."

"What?" I said.

Jessi

"The mystery notebook," Mallory repeated. "You know, the one I helped put together from all the notes about the other mysteries in our club notebook, remember? When we were being followed by that stalker?"

"I remember. But how is that going to help you solve this mystery? Do you already have a suspect? Someone we know about and made notes on? If you do, I can look it up for you."

"No," said Mallory, sounding surprised. "Where did you get that idea?"

"Because you said having the notebook would help you solve the mystery." It was my turn to sound a little impatient.

"Well, of course. We have to make notes in the notebook to solve the mystery, don't we? I mean, what am I supposed to do? Keep a list of clues in my social studies notebook?"

"It doesn't matter where you write the clues down to solve the mystery," put in Shannon.

She was right, of course.

But Mal was having none of it.

"No," she insisted. "I *have* to have the notebook. Listen. Coach Wu's husband is supposed to drive up with Mr. Blake's wife to join us for the weekend. Can you give the notebook to them, and they can bring it to me?"

I gave up. "Will do," I said. "Meanwhile, I

guess you'll have to keep the mystery notes on inn stationery, or something."

"Wellll . . . okay," said Mal. "I guess it will be all right, as long as I can transfer all the notes to the notebook just as soon as it gets here."

"Call if you need any more help with the mystery," I said. "Anything at all."

"No, that should do it," Mal said happily, and hung up.

Shannon was laughing when she came back into the kitchen. "Sorry, Jessi," she said, as we returned to putting out snacks. "I don't mean to laugh at Mal. I can tell she's really excited about this, and I'm sure I would be, too. It's just that she sounded as obsessed with that book as Jordan is with his spell book."

"I know," I answered. "I guess we have our hands full right here." When the Pikes had assembled around the table a few minutes later, I looked around. "Where's Nicky?"

"Still in his room," replied Margo.

Shannon stood up, ready to go find him, but was stopped when Nicky burst into the kitchen, holding something high. "I found it! I found it! Another five-dollar penny! The spell Jordan cast worked. It worked!"

Claire leaped up, her cardboard wings (now a riot of colors) flapping crazily. "I'm going to fly!" she announced. "Wheee!"

Jessi

It took a few minutes to restore order. The fact that Jordan folded his arms smugly and just sat there with a "See, I told you so" look on his face didn't help.

When everyone had calmed down and was more or less refocused on their snacks, Shannon and I exchanged glances. Then I cleared my throat. "You do know that you can't really cast a spell, don't you, Jordan?"

We gave the Pikes the "There is no such thing as a magic spell" speech. But we weren't sure we succeeded.

After all, how could we argue with a five-dollar penny?

CHAPTER 9

Kristy

Friday

Have I mentioned that Alan is a cretin? A brat? A lower, alien life form in barely human disguise?

He'd nailed me again. I should have seen it coming, but I didn't. After breakfast, we assembled with our buddies, plus Mrs. Bernhardt and our local guide, and walked to the House of the Seven Gables. As we walked, the guide pointed out the Salem Maritime National Historic Site. "Although Salem is most famous, or perhaps infamous, for the Witch Trials of sixteen ninety-two, don't forget that in the seventeen hundreds it was known throughout the world as a port of trade," she told us. "In fact, it was the sixth largest port in this country." The guide showed us the Custom House, where Nathaniel Hawthorne once worked, and told us that our admission fee to the House of the Seven Gables historic site would be used for the upkeep of the house, and to support a settlement house that helps people in the neighborhood. "Old and retired sailors, by the way, were known as old salts, from having been on the salty seas for so long," she informed us.

Mal whipped out her notebook and scribbled away. When we arrived, Mal counted the gables just to make sure there were seven. She wasn't the only one. We toured the house itself (where we learned that Nathaniel Hawthorne never actually lived there, but he used to visit his cousin

Susannah Ingersoll, who did) and the other cool old houses that were part of the site.

On the way back to the inn, we convinced Mrs. Bernhardt and the guide that we *had* to check out a local candy store. I was surveying the trays of chocolate behind the glass (and thinking that it was too bad Claudia wasn't with us) when Alan said, "Wow. Free samples!" He scooped one up into his mouth and passed a little dish to me. It only had one chocolate on it. That should have tipped me off. But I wasn't thinking. I took the chocolate and put it in my mouth.

And spit it out in my hand again. "EE-UUUUWW!" I screeched. "That's disgusting! It's salty!"

Everyone in the store looked at me, and two women who had been standing next to me moved away with looks that said, "Kids. No manners!"

I was gagging, and groping for a napkin to put the disgusting salty gooey mass in so I could throw it away (and wipe my hands), when I realized that Alan was practically laughing his stupid head off.

A candy store clerk came bustling out from behind the counter, wiping his hands on his white apron. "Is everything okay?" he asked.

I was mortified. I swallowed hard, trying to

get the taste of salt out of my mouth and said, "Yes. I'm sorry. It was a, uh, flavor I'm allergic to." How could I explain that Alan had offered me a salted chocolate — and I had fallen for it?

I saw Mrs. Bernhardt looking over at me and forced myself to smile. At last the clerk went away and everyone stopped staring at me and went back to staring at the chocolates.

Spinning around to face Alan, I said, "You, you, you despicable worm."

Cary Retlin, who'd been leaning against the wall with his arms folded, watching the show, straightened up. "I guess this makes you an old salt, then, Kristy."

I turned my back on both of them and went outside to breathe Alan-and-Cary-free air. Mal came out to join me. "At least they didn't slip you one of those antique Gilbraltars," she said, referring to a kind of candy that was originally popular because it could survive long sea voyages. A jar of Gilbraltars, with a label explaining that the candy inside was 150 years old, had been on display in the shop.

"That is no consolation," I said. I brooded over the Alan problem all the way back to the inn.

Of course, things weren't any better there. As we walked up to the Salem Gables and saw the police car out front, I realized that I must have missed out on some kind of excitement, probably at the very moment I was being salted by Alan. It did *not* help my mood.

While the others giggled and pointed at the side of the police car, which featured the silhouetted witch on a broomstick that is part of Salem's town symbol, and Mrs. Bernhardt suggested that we all take a break in our rooms until it was time to meet downstairs for lunch, I charged up the stairs and into the inn.

"What happened?" I demanded. "What's going on?"

At the front desk, Mr. Hewson had opened the registration book for a funny-looking man to examine (I later found out that he was Detective Frizell, who had interviewed Abby and Mary Anne). He looked up at my outburst.

"There's a police car out front," I pointed out.

"We're conducting an investigation here," said the funny-looking man severely.

"Of what?" I asked.

Mr. Hewson was about to answer, but Detective Frizell cut him off. "There has been a theft, and some clues may have turned up here at the inn. Now if you'll excuse us."

"A couple of classmates of yours found the clues," said Mr. Hewson, refusing to be intimidated by the detective. He smiled at me. "Mary Anne and . . . Abby, I think it was."

"Thanks," I said, and headed for our rooms at top speed, with Mal behind me.

Stacey, Mary Anne, and Abby were gathered in Stacey and Abby's room when I burst in.

"Hey, it's our fearless leader," said Abby.

"You'll never guess what's going on," said Mary Anne.

"A robbery," I said. "What's missing? Have they dusted for prints? Do they have any suspects? What clues did you guys find?"

"Whoa," said Abby.

"How did you know?" asked Mary Anne, looking a little disappointed.

I slowed down a little and grinned. "Cop car out front. So I asked Mr. Hewson what was up, and he told me that much. Elementary, my dear Spier."

"Agatha Kristy strikes again," murmured Abby. It was a nickname she'd stuck me with during our winter ski mystery.

"But he didn't tell me everything," I added.

By then, Mallory had caught up with me. She came into the room, closed the door, and sat down on one of the chairs. "Did you know that the Witch's Eye is missing?" she demanded.

"Yes!" Abby, Stacey, and Mary Anne chorused.

"The Witch's Eye!" I yelled. "Why didn't you tell me?"

"We're trying," said Abby. "But we're not telling you anything else until both of you quiet down and let us talk."

Mal and I shut up immediately.

When they'd finished, Mal said, "Why didn't I bring the mystery notebook? If we had it, we could write the clues down in it."

I brushed that aside. "You didn't see anybody leaving the museum, Mary Anne? Stacey? Nobody in a maintenance worker's uniform?"

They both shook their heads.

"And nobody has any idea what the numbers mean?" I continued.

"No, but I think they must be some kind of code," said Stacey.

Folding my arms, I announced, "I declare this an emergency meeting of the Baby-sitters Club. We have a mystery to solve."

"Why would the thief hide his — or her — clothes in the bushes outside the inn?" asked Abby. "Unless they wanted to come inside wearing normal clothes?"

"That means that they are either visiting someone here or staying here," I said.

"I vote for staying here," said Stacey. "It fits. Trove House is practically right next door. No getaway cars, a perfect disguise as an upright

Kristy

guest. Plus, those numbers were written on inn stationery."

We all nodded. Then Abby picked up the phone.

"What're you doing?" I asked.

"Calling the front desk to see if anyone checked out today."

Abby asked a few questions, listened, then hung up. "No new check-ins since we arrived. And no check-outs."

"I need the notebook to write all this down," sighed Mal. Then she brightened. "I know — I'll call Jessi and Shannon. They're baby-sitting at my house this afternoon. They can send the notebook to me with Mr. Wu and Mrs. Blake."

"Good idea, Mallory," I said absently. Then I said, "What about your newspaper spy? You know, that guy Stacey saw, who came into the room where the Witch's Eye had been and flashed some kind of i.d.? Where does he fit in?"

That distracted Mallory for a moment. "I don't know. But if the police let him in, he couldn't be the criminal."

"Unless he's in disguise," suggested Abby. "Maybe he, um, killed the real guy and then stole his identity. Happens all the time."

"Yeah, right, Abby," I said.

"Well, if the police let him in, he can't be *high*

on our list of suspects," Mallory mused. "But I'll leave him on it, just as soon as I make the list of suspects."

"How about that guy who tried to buy the diamond?" said Stacey. "Harvey Hapgood? Maybe he's so desperate for it that he stole it."

"Yeah. Harvey Hapgood. Sure! He's obsessed with it," said Abby, going off on another roll. "It haunts him day and night. He can't live without it. It's gotta be. Happens —"

"All the time," the rest of us chorused.

"Or the old double-cross," Abby went on.

"I can't wait," I muttered.

"Mrs. Moorehouse stole the diamond," Abby said.

"Not if she didn't have insurance," countered Mary Anne. "And from what I overheard, she doesn't. Besides, she's in a wheelchair. Even in a maintenance worker's uniform, she'd be noticeable."

"She's just faking!" persisted Abby. "How do we know she really can't walk? Her nurse knows, because she's not really a nurse. They're in it together."

We were all silent. It could be a possibility — except for that insurance thing.

Unless Mrs. Moorehouse wasn't telling the truth about the insurance. Maybe it wasn't Mrs.

Kristy

Moorehouse and Ms. Furusawa. Maybe it was Mrs. Moorehouse and someone else.

We talked over the theft until it was time to go down to lunch, and then we talked it over some more. Because naturally, that was what everyone was talking about — the theft of the Witch's Eye.

When the whole SMS group had been seated for lunch, Mr. Blake made an announcement about the theft. He said he knew we'd all heard about it, and that he didn't think it would interfere too much with our trip, though the Trove House Museum, unfortunately, would have to remain closed for awhile. "If this presents a problem for any of you, in terms of your history projects, please let me know. Otherwise, let's all try to carry on normally," he said.

Of course, the room was abuzz before he even sat down. It's amazing how fast rumors can spread. Long before lunch was over, we'd been told that a partial fingerprint had been found, a roadblock had been set up, and the police had sent the maintenance uniform to the FBI for analysis. How much of it was true? Who knew? Sitting in the dining room was like playing telephone — you know, that game in which you whisper something quickly in a person's ear, and they pass it along the same way, and at the end of the chain, the last person says what she

94

or he has heard. It usually has no resemblance to the original sentence.

I kept a sharp eye on Alan, but he was as caught up in the excitement as everybody else. The dining room of the inn remained a prank-free zone, at least for the moment.

It did not, however, remain cruelty-free. And I'm not talking about the fact that meat was served (sorry, Dawn). I'm talking about Cokie and Grace and their ongoing torment of Eileen.

Eileen was sitting silently, almost alone at her table. Before the trip, she'd been one of those quiet kids who sits with the other quiet kids. But now the other quiet kids were melting away, unwilling to be lumped in with her and included in Cokie's nasty jibes.

Eileen kept her head down when Cokie and Grace and their latest herd of sheep stopped at her table. "Who do you think stole the Witch's Eye, Eileen?" asked Cokie in a loud voice.

Staring at her almost untouched plate of food, Eileen shrugged.

"You don't know? I thought maybe you were riding over the museum on your broomstick when the theft occurred, and saw whoever did it sneaking out." Cokie swept out of the room on a wave of evil laughter.

"Cokie should be buried at a crossroads with a stake in her heart," muttered Abby.

"If you're implying that Cokie is a witch, forget it," I said. "I think you're insulting witchkind."

"Well, calling her human is insulting human-kind," said Mary Anne unexpectedly. We all looked at her in mild shock. Mary Anne almost never says anything nasty about anyone, because she always believes the best of people, even people like Cokie, who has done her utmost to make Mary Anne feel rotten.

Mal said slowly, "It is too bad that Eileen is so weird. It makes her an easy target." She stopped talking abruptly as Eileen rose from her table and walked past us out of the dining room. Then Ms. Garcia came over to our table. She was holding her five-year-old daughter's hand. "Mary Anne, I want to call on your baby-sitting skills this afternoon if I may. Since the whole group is going to walk along the Essex pedestrian mall and participate in some of the Haunted Happenings activities, will you take charge of Nidia for me?"

"Sure," replied Mary Anne. "Now?"

"If it is not too much trouble. We're going to be assembling in the lobby in just a few minutes and I'm going to need to keep my attention focused on maintaining order."

Mary Anne smiled at Nidia. "Hi, Nidia. Want to stay with me for awhile?" Nidia nodded and transferred her hand from her mother's to Mary Anne's without hesitation.

"Wow," I said. "Most kids are kind of shy with strangers."

"Not Nidia," said Ms. Garcia. "Since there are just the two of us, she's learned to be more self-reliant than most five-year-olds. And she's just naturally friendly, too, like her father was." She ran her hands lightly over Nidia's short curls and said, "I won't be far away, Nidia, okay?"

"Okay," agreed Nidia.

With Nidia in tow, we went out to cruise the bewitching streets of Salem. All kinds of amazing things were going on. Storytellers were telling tales of Old Salem; fortune-tellers were reading palms and tarot cards. And we saw several people wearing "Ask a Witch" buttons. They weren't really witches, of course, but people who could give answers to questions about the history of Salem, particularly the part pertaining to the famous witch trials. A lot of SMS kids stopped to question the "witches." Watching them, I suddenly remembered that I — like everyone else on this trip — was supposed to be pulling together a history project. I'd been so caught up in stewing about the Witch's Eye that I hadn't given my schoolwork much thought.

Hoping for inspiration, I ducked into a bookstore that appeared to be overflowing with books. Mal came along. She wanted to check for blank notebooks, "just in case," and she ended up adding two more books about Salem to her collection. She also bought a copy of *The House of the Seven Gables.* It was at the front of the store, in a display of books about Salem — the witch trials and the town in general.

"Look," I said to Mallory. "They have copies of *The Crucible.*" I picked one up and flipped through it. The play was being staged as part of the Salem Halloween celebration. Our group was going to see it that night. I looked at the man behind the counter. "This is a great bookstore," I said.

"Thanks," he replied. As he made change for Mallory, he continued, "You know, some people come in and see our books about the witch trials and tell me how awful it is that I'm selling 'books like that.' I've actually had people say to me, 'Where I come from, you wouldn't be allowed to sell such evil books.'"

I was outraged. "That's censorship. Or something."

He nodded. "I know. But I just tell them that I'm glad they live wherever they live, and not here."

Mal and I both laughed. We said good-bye

and went out to find the others. We located Stacey, Mary Anne, and Nidia at a face-painting booth. Nidia was having her face painted like a cat's. "I'm going to be a cat at the parade tomorrow night," she announced.

"I thought the parade was in the afternoon," said Stacey in surprise. "The children's costume parade." She nodded toward a sign listing all the events for the Haunted Happenings.

Just then, Abby appeared. "Nidia's right," she said. "There's another parade — for grownups, I guess — tomorrow evening."

"I'm there," I declared.

"Me, too," said Abby.

"Do you think it will be okay with Mrs. Bernhardt and the others?" Mary Anne asked anxiously.

"We can ask, but I bet they'll say yes. As long as we promise it won't interfere with our projects," Mal said.

Stacey bought a shirt that said "Boo" on it (for Claudia, she said), and Abby bought a little gold key chain with a clip for her pet pumpkin. We had to go back to the inn much too soon. But the play started at seven, and the inn was preparing a special New England boiled dinner for us beforehand. Plus, we were supposed to take some time to do research. Mal dashed into her room and called her house, to ask Jessi and Shannon to send the mystery notebook. Mary Anne and I read for awhile, and then we all dressed up (sort of — I put on corduroys and my best oxford shirt and a sweater vest). Naturally, we started talking about the mystery again while we were getting ready. Everybody agreed that we'd have to keep our eyes and ears open for clues, especially during dinner, when the dining room would be full of potential suspects.

Nothing unusual happened, though. And the New England boiled dinner was just that — everything boiled. But I bravely refrained from making the sort of comments I usually make over food at our school cafeteria. After a brief talk about the play, which was written by Arthur Miller, Mr. Baker handed out our theater tickets and then, since everything in Salem seems to be within walking distance, we walked to the theater.

I hate to admit this, but at the theater, Alan got me again, and I still haven't figured out how he did it. All I know is that everyone else handed their tickets over to ushers and went to sit down. But when the usher started escorting me to *my* seat, we ended up in the back corner of the theater. She frowned down at the ticket. "If we go any further," she muttered, "we'll be out in the parking lot." She trained a flashlight on my ticket, peered at it intently, and then said, "Someone's tampered with this."

She looked at me, and I felt my face turn red. "Alan," I gasped. "Oh, is he ever going to pay. What a major rat."

The usher laughed. "There's one in every school," she said. She studied the ticket a moment longer, then said, "I see where you are really supposed to be."

We walked back down the aisle, and she pointed me toward a seat by Abby.

"Good grief," I muttered, after thanking the usher and sliding into my seat (I only had to crawl over about a dozen people, since I was so late). As the lights went down, I heard Alan's familiar snicker somewhere over my right shoulder. I turned to make sure he wasn't too close. He made a face, and I made one back in spite of myself. But at least I knew he was six rows back and out of mischief-making distance.

Once the play began, I didn't think about Alan, or the Witch's Eye, or anything else. It was totally absorbing. *The Crucible* is all about the Salem Witch Trials, and how innocent people were convicted of things they didn't do, many of them because they wouldn't lie and confess or go along with the crowd in condemning others who were different.

Mary Anne cried.

Stacey said soberly, as we headed toward the lobby, "Wow. I'm never going to make jokes about witches again. That whole thing was *so* awful. I never realized."

"What an amazing play," Mal put in. "Arthur Miller is *such* a talented writer."

"It really makes you think, about *all* kinds of prejudice," Mary Anne said, between sniffs.

We drifted out to the front of the theater, talking in hushed voices. Suddenly Abby careened dramatically out of the door of the ladies room. I hadn't even noticed that she wasn't with us.

"Abby?" said Mallory. "What's wrong?"

Abby stopped staggering. She straightened up and grinned. "Nothing," she said. "Except that someone gave me a full body block, coming out of the bathroom. Good thing I'm a soccer player. I slammed her back."

"Did you see who it was?" I asked.

Abby shrugged. "Nah." She held up her ceramic pumpkin. "Maybe she didn't think I should be allowed to take pets into the bathroom."

"Or maybe you just bought yourself a bad-luck pumpkin."

102

"Shhh." Abby cupped her hand around the pumpkin. "Cornucopia might hear you."

"Cornucopia?" asked Mallory.

"That's what I call my new pet," explained Abby.

I groaned and rolled my eyes. Sometimes, Abby can be *so* weird.

Claudia

Friday

Do I have any costume sugestions? Of corse I do! I just wish I could be in Salim to ware a costume in the parade myself.

I WISH I COULD BE IN SALEM, TOO, CLAUDIA.

Ooh, Mary Anne, Logan misses you.

When Stacey called on Friday night, I was hunched over my homework, brooding deeply. Homework! On a Friday night! Okay, so it was homework I was doing over, and I suppose I should have been glad that my teacher was letting me rethink some of my answers in math. But gratitude was not what I was feeling.

"Stacey!" I gasped when I heard her voice. "You've saved my life." Before she could say anything else, I'd launched into some of the more puzzling aspects of my recycled math homework.

Stacey listened. She made suggestions. She explained. The appearance (and correctness) of my homework improved considerably.

I wrote the answer to the last question and sighed with relief. Then I remembered what Jessi and Shannon had told me, about their phone call from Mal.

"STACEY!" I shrieked. "What's happening? Tell me *everything*!"

"What?" said Stacey. "I can't hear you. I think you blew out my eardrum."

I took the hint and softened my voice. "New clues? New suspects?"

"Not yet," said Stacey. She told me that they thought the thief must be someone who was still in the hotel, since no one had checked out.

Claudia

That made sense. No arrests had been made, but Stacey had heard that the police didn't want any of the guests leaving Salem yet.

I was beginning to feel deeply envious that they were in Salem having all the excitement when Stacey told me about the Halloween parade.

"We need costume suggestions, Claud," she concluded.

I immediately felt better. And less left out. "Costumes," I said. "Wow. We'll have to work around what you guys took with you. Describe your traveling wardrobes, please."

We spent a very satisfying half hour going over the possibilities. We came up with some decent costume ideas which would require only face paint, makeup, and paper bags, augmented (see, I learn my vocabulary words even if I can't spell them) by a few small purchases from the local stores.

"Be sure to take a photo," I said. "Take many. Maybe I will make a Salem collage after all."

"I will," promised Stacey.

"And call me *instantly* if you find any new clues or solve the mystery."

"Done," Stacey vowed. She said good-bye and we hung up. I stared down at my homework for a moment. For tonight, at least, I'd fought my homework and I'd won. But it had

106

seemed extra-hard. And I'd really needed Stacey's help. I hoped this didn't mean I had more school troubles ahead.

School. I made a face. It was the weekend, I told myself. My math homework was done, at least. I wasn't going to think about school anymore that night. I decided to read a Nancy Drew book and do some junk food munching — two things that go together perfectly, if you ask me.

On Saturday morning, Logan and I were sitting for a combined Brewer/Thomas/Papadakis group, all assembled at Kristy's house. Since the day was gray, we were gathered indoors. "I hope it doesn't rain tomorrow," said Karen anxiously. "Tomorrow is Halloween."

"It's not going to rain," said Hannie Papadakis. She is one of Karen's best friends. They are the same age and go to school together at Stoneybrook Academy.

"Good," said Karen. "Because if it does, and you bump into a real ghost on Halloween while it is, then you will melt."

Her brother Andrew, who is four and somewhat sensitive, immediately looked frightened.

"That's not true," said Logan firmly.

"It could be true," suggested Karen.

"Not on this planet," insisted Logan.

That made Andrew smile.

"So we're stuck inside today, right?" asked Linny Papadakis. Linny is nine and a good friend of Kristy's seven-year-old brother David Michael.

"Yup," said Logan cheerfully.

"We could play hide-and-seek," suggested Linny.

"Yes!" Karen's eyes widened behind her glasses and she held up her hands like claws. "And to make it exciting, we can jump out and go 'boo'! That will make it Halloween Hide-and-Seek."

"Uh, no," I said firmly, seeing Andrew hunch his shoulders. I thought for a moment and then asked, "Does everyone have a costume for Halloween?"

Of course, everybody did. For the next few minutes Logan and I were swamped with descriptions of who was wearing what.

"Whoa," I said. "I wish I had known all this when I talked to Stacey last night."

"Stacey is in Salem, Massachusetts," Karen explained importantly. "For a school trip. They traveled on a bus and they are staying overnight in an inn. An inn is an old house that is like a hotel, except probably haunted."

"The Salem Gables Inn is *not* haunted," I interrupted, trying not to laugh.

"But it could be," said Karen.

Logan and I exchanged glances, and made a mutual decision to let that go.

"Because if I'd known what great costumes you all had," I continued, "it would have helped me come up with ideas for costumes for Kristy and Stacey and Mallory and Abby."

"Costumes? Why do *they* need costumes?" asked Hannie.

"Salem is having a big Halloween parade this year," I explained, "and all the SMS kids are going to be in it."

Karen practically levitated. "A parade? A parade!" she squeaked. "I want to be in a Halloween parade!"

"Me, too!" cried Hannie.

"Me, too," said Andrew softly.

Almost instantly all the other kids joined in.

"Hey," I said.

Everyone kept talking at once.

"Hey!"

Everyone talked louder.

Logan put two fingers in his mouth and whistled.

That made everyone quiet down. "Thank you, ladies and gentlemen," Logan said. Once again, he and I exchanged glances. Then he continued, "And now that I have your undivided attention,

Claudia

Claudia and I have an announcement to make."
He bowed in my direction and Karen giggled.

I bowed back. Then I said, "We'd like to an-
nounce that there is no reason you can't have a
Halloween parade of your own."

Cheers broke out, and then all the talking began again. Logan whistled once more.

"We can't plan a parade if everybody talks at
once. We need to organize this. Who wants to
take notes?"

"I will," offered Linny.

"Good. The Stoneybrook Halloween Parade
Planning Committee will meet in the den in . . ."
Logan looked at his watch. "Three minutes."

A stampede broke out for the den. Soon Logan
and I were refereeing a parade brainstorming
session, which was not very different from utter
chaos. Suggestions flew, arguments erupted, ri-
valries over who was going to lead and who
was going to follow broke out. But by the time
Watson could be heard coming in the front door,
a route (along the street to the nearby park), a
meeting place (Watson's mansion), a time (afternoon, "so people can take lots of pictures"), and
a phone chain (to notify everybody else the kids
wanted to involve) had been set up.

"Daddy, Daddy!" shrieked Karen dramatically. "You have a very important job."

"What's his job, Karen?" I asked, as she

110

jumped up and prepared to race down the front hall to her father.

"He has to fix it so we can march down the middle of the street with *no* cars," said Karen, and flew out of the room.

"Well," I said. "It looks like we're going to have a parade. I just hope it doesn't rain on it!"

"Yeah," Logan grinned. "I'd hate to be standing next to a real ghost — and be washed away!"

CHAPTER 11

Abby

I blame it all on my Saturday Pet Pumpkin, of course. If it had been a better watch-pumpkin, instead of a bad-luck pumpkin, maybe I wouldn't have been at the center of a Halloween parade crime wave....

Mallory snatched her notebook from Mr. Wu's hand as if it were a life preserver. "Thank you," she said.

Over her shoulder, I could see that Jessi had not only put the notebook in an envelope and taped every possible opening shut, but she had also written *Personal* and *Confidential* all over it.

Talk about making something look conspicuous.

We'd spent a quiet morning in the local library doing research for our school projects. In addition to our short individual reports, all of us were going to make a map of Salem to be put on display at SMS. We were going to label and illustrate the things we thought were interesting and important.

I'd honestly been suspicious of this morning in the library. I mean, *all* of us together? With creeps like Alan and lightweights like Cokie and Grace, how could anybody get any work done?

Never underestimate the power of a librarian's glare, especially when combined with the unexpected grasp of a teacher's hand on your shoulder. Coach Wu swooped down on Cokie after the second giggle and that was the last we heard from her. And interestingly enough, Mrs. Bernhardt managed to be very near Alan at all times, even when he drifted into the stacks to do research.

As a result, I got a lot more work done than I expected (and I think some other people did, too, in spite of themselves), and I was looking forward to the quiet time after lunch and before the parade. I didn't see how Kristy and some of the others could jump to attention when Mr. Blake suggested yet one more "quick" sight-seeing excursion. Nor could I understand how Mallory could get so intense over the mystery notebook.

But she did.

Turning to me with the notebook pressed against her chest, Mallory declared, "I'm going into the inn library to work on this and bring it up to date."

"Whatever," I said. I stifled a yawn and thought about a nap. "Don't forget that the little kids' parade is this afternoon."

"I know. And I haven't forgotten that Mary Anne is baby-sitting for Nidia tonight during the grown-ups' parade. I haven't forgotten *anything*," Mallory said earnestly. "And it's all about to go in this book." She gave it a pat.

"Okay, Mal. We'll come get you when it's

time for the kids' parade and the shopping expedition."

Mallory nodded and charged down the hall
that led from the main entrance of the inn to the
library at the back.

I turned in a more dignified manner (another
yawn) and went upstairs to my room, stopping
to call out to Mary Anne, who was playing on
the swings with Nidia.

Several outfits were scattered across Stacey's
bed, and the sound of splashing and the per-
fumy smell of bubble bath told me that she was
submarining around in the bathtub.

"It's me," I said (in case she hadn't guessed). I
hung the *Do Not Disturb* sign on the door,
stretched out on the bed, and zonked out.

I woke up to Stacey saying, "Abby! It's time
to go shopping."

"Shopping?" I sat up and yawned. "What
happened to the kids' parade?"

"That, too," said Stacey impatiently. "But
Mrs. Bernhardt just came around and told
everyone that if you don't want to watch the parade, you can come with the group and have
some time to shop at the pedestrian mall."

"I'm joyous," I said, sitting up. "I better go get
Mal. She's probably still in the library."

She was. Her fingers were stained with ink

115

and her glasses were crooked. She was bent over the notebook writing with such concentration that when I touched her shoulder she jumped.

"Showtime," I said.

"Oh. Oh, right." Mal straightened her glasses and closed the notebook carefully.

The entire SMS group was going to turn out for the grown-ups' parade that night, and at least half the group wanted to go out and buy things for their costumes.

Fortunately Ms. Garcia and Nidia weren't the only ones going to the children's parade that afternoon. Coach Wu and Mr. Wu were going, too, along with Mrs. Bernhardt, while the tireless Blake family went on yet another sightseeing excursion, this time to the Witch House, which isn't the house where an alleged witch once lived, but the house of one of the judges in the Salem Witch Trials.

We walked to the pedestrian mall and Mr. and Mrs. Blake herded their group (including Kristy) away. The place was swarming with little kids and more were pouring in every second.

Stacey gave the crowd a quick once-over and took charge. Good thing, too. I'm not a big shopper. Stacey, of course, is practically a professional. Mallory and Mary Anne are about average, I suspect. They don't mind shopping, but they don't go out of their way to do it.

The Essex Street Mall, which is for pedestrians only, isn't very long but there are more than enough places to shop. Coach Wu told us we had to stay together in pairs (the old buddy system rears its ugly head), we couldn't leave the mall area, and we had to meet back by the side entrance of the Peabody Essex Museum in one hour.

Everyone scattered (in twos) but we hadn't gone ten steps before the kids leading the children's parade appeared. Mary Anne and Mallory made a U-turn to head back, oohing and ahhing over how cute they all were.

"Look," exclaimed Mary Anne. "There's Nidia! She's a cat."

"We already knew that," I pointed out. "She walked over here with us."

Just then, Nidia saw us and smiled and waved.

"And a *very* cute cat," I added. "The cutest one in the parade."

We watched the parade as if we had never seen kids in costumes before. Until Stacey looked at her watch and switched back into her consumer mode. "Uh-oh," she said. "We have less than forty minutes left to do our shopping. Let's go!"

We finished just as the parade was ending, and ran into Martha Kempner in the shoe store where we'd stopped to make a special sock purchase. She smiled and waggled her fingers at us, then returned her attention to her feet, which were strapped into silvery open-toed sandals with very high heels.

Stacey whispered, "Well, they make her legs look longer."

"Yeah." I snorted. "And those shoes are going to make her into a cripple if she keeps wearing them. Do you have any idea what high heels do to your feet, your legs, your back, your whole body? I mean, if men had to wear shoes like that, how long do you think high heels would be fashionable?"

"We're not here to talk about the politics of shoes," said Mary Anne hesitantly.

Mal said loyally, "Martha — Ms. Kempner always looks great."

"I'm surprised she can think with those instruments of torture on her feet. No wonder she writes books about murder," I said.

We made it back to the meeting place with nine seconds to spare. I know it was nine seconds because Kristy was there, keeping time.

We spent the rest of the afternoon working on

our costumes for the adult parade that evening, with a quick break for dinner before we went upstairs to make ourselves parade-worthy. When we emerged from our rooms afterward, in full regalia, we looked outstanding — a tribute to Claudia's genius, our own ingenuity, and the wonders of recycling.

Kristy was wearing her collie cap (which is in memory of her dog Louie, who died), a necklace made of dog biscuits and bones, and one of those fake nose-moustache-glasses combinations, and carrying a large magnifying glass. She was also wearing a name tag that said "Sherlock Bones."

Mallory, dressed almost entirely in orange (including a Day-Glo orange down vest of mine), had pinned cut-out paper pumpkins all over her body, connected with green yarn. She was wearing the top half of one of those hollow plastic pumpkins as a hat and carrying the pumpkin itself, from which trailed green yarn and paper leaves. She had borrowed my pet pumpkin and clipped it to her belt loop. What was Mallory? You mean you couldn't tell? A pumpkin patch!

Mary Anne was going as her kitten, Tigger. She wore whiskers and ears made of felt and mittens with fake fingernails trimmed into claws. The outfit was topped (or bottomed) off with a tail made of yarn attached to one of Kristy's gray sweatshirts.

Stacey had fallen back on her assortment of basic black clothing. Dressed in black from head to toe, she had painted her face with the numbers of a clock. She was Mother Time.

My costume description comes last because I consider it the best — not Claudia's idea, although Claudia inspired it (she'd suggested a soccer theme to me). I was wearing my shirt that read, "Soccer: Invented by men, perfected by women." I had also attached one of those plastic blow-up globes to one shoulder and a plastic cup to the other. I was the women's soccer World Cup, get it?

No one did except me. But that was okay. I don't mind being the only one around smart enough to laugh at my own jokes.

When Ms. Garcia saw Mary Anne's costume, she grinned hugely. "A big cat and a little cat. I'll have to take a picture of this for my album." Nidia, naturally, was delighted, too. It was quite a cute-fest to see the two cool cats together. Mary Anne was in charge of Nidia during the adult parade, so that Ms. Garcia could keep an eye on all of us.

Salem was overflowing with people. Halloween is a huge celebration there. As our SMS group edged out of the house into the crowds of ghosts and ghouls, I heard Cokie start ragging on Eileen again.

"Like my costume, Eileen?" she asked.

I heard Eileen murmur, "No." I didn't have to turn around to agree. I'd checked out Cokie and Grace earlier. They were dressed as witches (how original) in stereotypical costumes: pointed hats, elaborate costumes, red nails. They were even carrying brooms.

"What an *interesting* costume you have on, Eileen. What are you supposed to be?" Cokie prodded her.

"I'm not wearing —"

"You'll have to show us how to fly these things later." Cokie and Grace both cackled. Literally. That's how they always laugh.

People like Cokie and Grace were probably the ones who gave witches a bad name to begin with.

Suddenly Mallory edged in beside Eileen, who, having been singled out from the herd, was now being ignored by everyone. She grabbed Eileen's elbow and said, "Come on, Eileen. Let's get near the front where we can see." With that, she dragged Eileen out of Cokie's range.

"Blood," a creepy voice nearby intoned. "Blooooooood."

"Get lost, Alan," I heard Kristy say.

Abby

Alan was dressed as a vampire.

Cary was wearing whiskers, a long pointed nose, furry ears, and had somehow attached patches of fake fur to his cheeks. "Rat man," he kept explaining with a rodent smile.

The parade was awesome. The street was jammed. Even if cars had been allowed to drive on it, they wouldn't have fit. Ahead I saw Mary Anne take Nidia's hand. Nidia pressed close to Mary Anne the way a kitten does to a mother cat.

We were on the buddy system again, and had decided on a meeting place if we got separated. But the teachers were keeping a pretty sharp eye on everyone, trying to prevent that from happening. Frankly, I was glad of it. The crowd surged and pressed around us with a life of its own, and if I'd been by myself, it might have been scary.

"Alan! Get away!" I heard Kristy say, and then I heard her howl with rage.

Alan slithered by and I instinctively stuck out my foot. Under normal conditions, he would have gone sprawling, but the crowd had become so thick that he just reeled sideways against someone before rebounding.

He turned and stuck out his tongue at me. "Fangs a lot," he said and oozed away.

Kristy appeared, spitting on her hand and rubbing her neck. Two red dots glittered there.

For one moment, I thought Alan had actually bitten her. And of course, that meant she'd have to get rabies shots, I thought, only half joking with myself.

Then Kristy said, "It's permanent ink. It's probably going to stay on *forever.* He is such a jerk!"

Someone crashed against me and it was my turn to reel back. A voice said, "Hey, watch it, kid," and hands grabbed at my waist. I straightened up and turned and caught a glimpse of a white-sheeted figure disappearing into the crowd.

My hands dropped instinctively to my waist pack. Had I been mugged by a ghost? Had my pocket been picked by a poltergeist?

I looked down in disbelief. I had. My instincts had been correct. The person in the ghost costume had nabbed my waist pack.

It was gone.

"Hey!" I shouted. "Hey!" I pushed forward, then stopped as the crowd pushed me back. I could see at least three ghosts in the immediate crowd, any one of whom might have been the pickpocket ghost. Like witches, ghosts were a very popular costume.

"Hey!" I shouted again, this time in frustration. I raised my voice. *"Everyone be careful! There is a pickpocket in a ghost costume here!"*

Abby

No one even seemed to notice except Stacey, who as my buddy wasn't supposed to get separated from me. "You had your pocket picked?" she exclaimed, turning toward me.

"Not picked — removed. Someone took my waist pack," I explained. My hands were shaking, thinking how easy it was for the robber. "Some creep in a sheet grabbed it, just like that."

"They must have cut the strap," she said, with a knowing nod of her head. "I've heard about that before."

"Oh, well, it's no big deal," I said, trying to calm down. It really wasn't, but it infuriated me that someone would do that. I took a deep breath. "It just had the key card to my room in it, and a couple of dollars. The key card isn't labeled or anything, so that's no problem."

"Still, you should report it to the police."

"Tomorrow, maybe, not tonight. Come on, we don't want to get left behind." I forced myself to laugh, and then felt better. "I guess I can't blame my pet pumpkin for this bad luck. I don't even have it. Mal does."

We hurried and caught up with the others.

Eventually, the parade had to go on without us. It was still growing in size, and the noise level was increasing exponentially, when we left to make our way back to the hotel. All kinds of ghosts and goblins were wandering the streets, and pumpkins leered from windows, Halloween flags snapped in the sharp air, silhouettes of witches and black cats could be seen outlined in the glass panels of doors and windows.

Salem really did get dressed up for Halloween. It was, I thought somewhat cynically, a big business in these parts. I wondered what the people who'd been killed for refusing to confess to being witches would think of all this. After all, it was their deaths that had given Salem the reputation it was capitalizing on now.

I stopped at the front desk to report the lost key, and Mr. Hewson promised me another first thing in the morning. I followed Stacey upstairs to our room.

She was standing in the doorway when I arrived, a silhouette in black against the light coming from the room. It was a very dramatic pose, both hands up to her face, her legs braced as if she were about to spring into action.

"Nice pose, Mother Time, but you'll have to move. I'm wiped out," I said.

Then my jaw dropped.

Our room was trashed. I mean, I'm not the neatest person in the world, but no way had I left it like that.

Abby

Totaled. Ransacked. Destroyed. Words like that (and a few worse ones) came to mind.

"I don't believe this," Stacey murmured, picking her way carefully into the room.

"Believe it," I said. I lifted my upended suitcase off the floor and set it down again. Where was I going to put it? My bed was completely torn apart. The mattress was off. The blankets were everywhere. The only thing the intruder hadn't done was rip the pillows. The dresser drawers had all been yanked out. Shoes were scattered across the floor. Stacey's jewelry box was open, lying on its side on the dresser.

"My jewelry," she said faintly. But a few minutes later she said in a puzzled voice, "It's all here. What about you, Abby? Are you missing anything?"

"Not that I can tell," I said. I travel pretty light, so unless the thief was interested in long underwear or sweats or something, he was out of luck.

Except for my money! My money! I'd left most of it in the room, in the bedside table. I hadn't taken it with me because I didn't want it to be stolen, foresight for which I had congratulated myself after my waist pack was snatched.

But it was still there, too, beneath the overturned drawer on the floor next to the bed.

"Whoa," said Kristy's voice from the doorway. "What's the deal here?"

"Oh, no!" Mary Anne's voice chimed in.

"I don't know," I said as Kristy stepped forward and helped me wrestle the mattress back into place, while Mary Anne did the same for Stacey. "But it doesn't look like a robbery. As far as we can tell, nothing is missing. No money, no jewelry."

"Why would someone do this?" Kristy frowned and put her hand up to rub at the two red "fang" marks on her neck.

"Not Alan," said Mary Anne. "Or Cary, either."

"Cokie and company?" I guessed.

Kristy shook her head. "No, not even Cokie. Besides, she has someone else to pick on right now."

"Plus," Stacey pointed out, "she couldn't get into this room. I mean, she's not a professional lock picker that I know of."

"Cary can get into locked things," said Kristy darkly.

Stacey said, "These rooms have electronically coded door locks, remember? Not even Cary could pick those."

"Yeah," Kristy conceded. "Besides, this isn't Cary's style. It's too, too . . ."

Abby

"Unsubtle," I suggested.

"And, much as I hate to admit it, it's too mean," said Kristy.

Mal looked in, sized up the situation, said, "Don't anybody move!" and disappeared. She reappeared a moment later holding the mystery notebook and a pen. Uprighting the desk chair, she sat down and began to take notes.

"You don't think this has something to do with the Witch's Eye, do you?" asked Mary Anne, shocked.

"Maybe. Maybe not. We can't take any chances of missing any clues."

"Well," I said, "Salem is certainly an *interesting* city. Purse snatchings. Room ransackings . . ." My voice trailed off. "Purse snatchings," I repeated. Naturally, I'd told everybody all about what had happened immediately, and we'd all kept a ghostwatch. But hadn't been approached again by any ghosts, suspicious or otherwise.

"My room key was in my waist pack," I said.

"But it wasn't labeled, was it?" Stacey asked. "Those card keys all look the same."

"It didn't need to be, if someone knew who I was and where I was staying."

"But how would they know, Abby?" asked Mary Anne.

"They could have seen it on the guest register," I said, thinking hard.

128

Mal looked up from the notebook. "Or they could be staying right next door."

"What? Mal, what are you talking about?" I demanded.

"Harvey Hapgood," she said simply. "I saw him just now. Coming out of the room next to yours."

CHAPTER 12

Mallory
😐

The Harvey Hapgood clue. Was there a connection? Was he spying on us? Did he know that Stacey had been in the museum, and think she had some kind of clue to where the diamond was? Some kind of clue that even she didn't know about? It didn't make sense. So we took some action that did make sense. We went down to the library for some of the late night hot chocolate that the inn offered.

By we, I mean the five of us plus Eileen. I went back to my room and invited her. I expected her to say no, but she didn't. Maybe it had something to do with the fact that we had been buddies in the parade. When she said yes, I wasn't sure I was entirely happy about it. Did being nice to her mean I was going to be teased by Cokie now, too?

I tried not to think about that, first because it was cowardly to care what someone like Cokie Mason said, and second because I had more important things to think about, such as the mystery of the Witch's Eye.

Mary Anne made a brief detour, to say good night to Nidia Garcia as she had promised. She also reported the break-in to Mrs. Garcia, who made sure the hotel changed the key code on the door.

Downstairs by the fire, we found Martha Kempner. She waved us over and said, "Great hot chocolate. Just what I needed after all that Halloween madness."

"Did you go to the parade?" asked Eileen. She was leaning forward, her face almost animated. I realized that in school, she often spoke up. But on this trip, Cokie's teasing had silenced her.

"Yes," replied Ms. Kempner. "I considered it part of my research, as well as a lot of fun."

"Are you still going to write your article on the Witch's Eye?" I asked. "I mean, now that it's missing?"

"Yes. I'm sorry, of course, that it is gone, but in a way, it will make this an even better story. After all, it certainly ties in with the curse."

Eileen spoke again. "The curse? There's a curse on the diamond?"

"Yes. It has a history of bad luck, of causing dire misfortune — even death — to all who encounter it."

"Just like my pumpkin," I heard Abby mutter.

Martha glanced her way, looking amused.

"Will you tell me about it? The curse?" I asked.

The amused look deepened. Ms. Kempner leaned forward, her mug of hot chocolate cradled in her hands, and stared into the fireplace at the leaping flames.

"Once upon a time, in Europe, long ago, a beautiful young woman was burned at the stake, put to death as a witch. Some say she was accused because she rejected the attentions of a rich and jealous suitor, preferring to stay single. Others said it was because of her eyes, which were an unusual pale golden brown. At any rate, when the fire was lit (they say) she called out a terrible curse. The fire roared up then, so brightly that no one could look at it. Then it died away. The stunned onlookers found that not a stick of wood had burned, and there was no sign of the woman at all.

"But lying among the strangely warm branches was a single large stone, a jewel such as none of the villagers had ever seen before.

"The rich suitor — a prince, perhaps — who had witnessed the affair, seized the jewel.

"Within days, his castle had burned to the ground, and everything in it was destroyed. The only thing that survived the terrible inferno was this single, blazing yellow stone. That was when the people began to call it the Witch's Eye, and to say that it was cursed.

"But as so often happens, greed overcame fear, and the prince's heirs claimed the stone. Soon after that, the family fortunes changed. The prince's heirs fell out of favor with the king, and lost nearly all they owned. They sold the diamond just in time, some said, or they might have lost their heads as well.

"After that, the diamond disappeared from sight, although it resurfaced from time to time, always in connection with some tragedy. Then a great uncle of Mrs. Moorehouse's discovered it when he bought a collection of costume jewelry in a dusty secondhand store in England just after World War One. It was the talk of the town. Some said the owner of the store went mad when he realized that he had sold a treasure for the price of a fake. It was written up in all the papers, but Mrs. Moorehouse's uncle knew its dark history and was taking no chances. He donated it to a museum for his lifetime, and there it stayed, doing no harm. Then he died not too long ago, and Mrs. Moorehouse inherited it."

"How much bad luck has she had?" Kristy asked. "Aside from having the diamond stolen, I mean."

"So far, none that I know of, aside from the theft," Ms. Kempner answered. She turned her gaze from the fire to the rest of us. "But no one knows what the exact nature of the curse was. Perhaps good people are exempt."

"*Not* like my pet pumpkin," said Abby.

Wow, I thought. I was impressed. The story was as good as one of Martha's mysteries. Even better, because it was true.

Martha leaned back and stretched. Then she looked at Abby. "That's your pet?" she asked, pointing to the pumpkin that dangled from the key chain clip attached to Abby's belt loop.

"Yeah. I have to keep it on a short leash," Abby joked.

"My goddaughter would love it, and I haven't really found her a souvenir of Salem yet. I always try to take her something from all my research trips. You wouldn't be interested in selling it, would you?"

"Sell my pet? How could I?" Folding her hands over her heart, Abby looked dramatically toward the ceiling. Then she returned to her, well, not normal but more *usual* mode and said, "But I bought it in the gift shop. I bet you could find another one there."

During Martha's telling of the story of the Witch's Eye, we'd all been so enthralled that we had barely noticed other people coming in for the hot chocolate, which was set up on a table across the room. Maybe simply talking about the Witch's Eye brings bad luck, too. Who knows?

At any rate, Alan struck again, this time with Cokie's help. And the target wasn't Kristy, but Eileen.

She suddenly jumped and cried, "Owww!"

She held up her hand. I could see a red mark on it. Another voice said, "A rat. It was a rat. A rat just bit Eileen."

Naturally, everyone screamed. Eileen leaped to her feet, her eyes wild.

Then Cokie's familiar, nasty voice said, "No. It was a cat. I saw it. A black cat. Isn't that funny? A witch, bitten by a black cat. I wonder if that will kill the cat."

"Alan!" exclaimed Kristy in disgust, her hand going to the two red marks on her neck.

"Of Transylvania," he said and gave one of his weird, stupid laughs. He was, as you have probably figured out, still in full vampire costume. He swooped his cloak up over his face and made a dramatic exit.

Eileen just stood there, her face white and her eyes still wide and shocked. She had placed one hand over the other. Now that we weren't all panicking, it was easy to see that the blood was fake.

Cokie just kept laughing. "You should see your face," she gasped. "You don't look like a witch, you look like a ghost."

"You, you," stammered Eileen. "I — you . . . why?" The last word ended in a wail, and she charged out of the room, almost knocking over Mary Anne, who was just coming in.

"Did you catch that look on her face?" Cokie said.

As an audience, we were not responsive. Then Kristy stood up. She looked positively menacing, even for the shortest person in the eighth grade. Kristy put her face up close to Cokie's and Cokie stopped laughing with a sharp little intake of breath.

"This time," said Kristy, "you've gone too far."

I suddenly found myself on my feet, too. "Leave Eileen alone, Cokie," I heard myself say.

Cokie switched her gaze from Kristy to me. She tried to sneer, but she didn't do her usual professional job of it. "Oh, yeah," she scoffed. "Says who?"

"Says me," I shot back.

"And me." Mary Anne stepped forward from where she had stood frozen by the door.

"And me," chorused Abby and Stacey, leaping to their feet at almost the same instant.

No one spoke. The fire crackled in the dimly lit room and I had a sudden vision of the people who had been charged with witchcraft facing their tormentors in just such dimly lit rooms long ago. What if someone had stood up then and said, "Stop." The Salem Witch Trials might never have happened.

Cokie took one step back, and then another. Then she raised her chin and, trying to act dignified (but failing), left.

We all stood in a sort of tableau for a moment longer. Then Abby said, "Well. This calls for some more hot chocolate. Mary Anne, you want some?"

We settled down and talked with Martha Kempner for a little while longer. She told us about other famous jewels that were said to be cursed, such as the Hope Diamond. Then she excused herself, saying she had more research to do. We watched as she tapped to the door on those amazing heels.

Mary Anne, who had grabbed the pillow next to me, sighed. "Wow, this has been some night," she said softly.

"You can say that again," I whispered back.

"Yeah, and on top of everything else, I think you were being spied on."

"What?"

"I'll tell you later."

And she did, as we were going up to our rooms. "Sean Knowles — the suspicious man with the newspaper we saw our first day here — and Harvey Hapgood were standing outside the open library door together when I came back from saying good night to Nidia," Mary Anne explained. "They were whispering. They might have been eavesdropping, but I'm not sure. Anyway, Sean Knowles looked into the library, and then said something that I didn't hear. When they turned to leave, I ducked into the alcove beneath the stairs there. I don't think they saw me."

"Do you really think they were spying on us? Why?" asked Kristy. "Too bad you couldn't hear what they said."

"I know," said Mary Anne.

The mystery was growing more mysterious

every moment. I went back to my room to write down this new clue — if it was a new clue. In a mystery like this one, who knew? Eileen was already in her nightgown and bathrobe. She ducked her head when I came in.

I suddenly wondered if that was what she had been doing since the beginning of the trip — ducking, trying to stay away from Cokie, planning every move she made in the hope of avoiding teasing and torment.

I said, "Cool story about the Witch's Eye, huh?"

Eileen glanced up warily. "Yes," she replied. "But I don't really believe in curses, even though one of my ancestors was accused of being a witch. She wasn't a witch, you know. She was innocent, like all the rest. And she didn't get hanged in the end."

"She outlasted the madness," I said, remembering what we had learned: that by 1693, less than a year after it had begun, the hysteria about witches had died down. Suddenly everyone was ashamed of what had happened. A few years after that, the young girl who had been the first to accuse others of witchcraft stood up in church and recanted.

"You don't believe the Witch's Eye is bad luck, do you?" asked Eileen.

"Well, it sounds as if it is," I answered. I remembered Jordan and his book of spells. "My brother Jordan would tell you that it had cast a spell on everyone. When I left Stoneybrook, he was going around pretending that he had found a real book of spells. He was casting them on everybody."

"He sounds funny. My little brother is funny, too, but that's because he is a baby, and babies can't help but be cute and funny."

We started talking about our families, and I realized that Eileen really wasn't all that weird. She was just a social klutz. And that was what made her such an easy target for Cokie and Grace, and even Alan. It was human nature to go after anyone who was different, and to protect oneself by hiding in the middle of a crowd, going along with everyone else.

The Salem Witch Trials were just one example of that pattern in history.

"Hey, it's getting late," I said at last. "And I have some work to do." (I let Eileen think it was for my trip project. I didn't tell her it was writing down new clues.) "But I'll wake you up to go to breakfast with us tomorrow, okay?"

"You sure?" asked Eileen.

"Absolutely," I said.

CHAPTER 13

LOGAN

SATURDAY

DEAR MARY ANNE,

BY THE TIME YOU READ THIS YOU
WILL BE BACK FROM SALEM. I HOPE
YOU ARE HAVING A GOOD TIME. IT
SOUNDS LIKE SOME AMAZING THINGS
ARE HAPPENING. SOME PRETTY AMAZ-
ING — OR AT LEAST AMAZINGLY
FUNNY — THINGS ARE HAPPENING
HERE, TOO . . . .

News of the parade spread among our clients like wildfire, as I found out when I reached the Rodowskys' for my sitting job. Not a single Rodowsky appeared to say hello when I rang the doorbell (that is, not a single kid — Mr. Rodowsky answered the door).

The Rodowsky adults passed along the usual information (phone numbers where they could be reached, estimated time of return, emergency contacts), and then headed out.

Still no sign of the junior Rodowskys.

"Mr. Rodowsky," I called out, just before he closed the front door behind him.

"Yes, Logan?"

"Where is everybody?"

He laughed. "In one of the boys' rooms."

"Working on a house-wide mess," added Mrs. Rodowsky with a smile. "A really scary one."

That made both the Rodowskys laugh, as if Mrs. Rodowsky had said something very witty.

Closing the door behind them, I went on a Rodowsky hunt and soon unraveled the mini-mystery, and the Rodowsky seniors' source of merriment.

The Rodowsky boys were making Halloween costumes. When I walked in, they had reached the papier-mâché stage.

By that, I don't mean they were actually working with papier-mâché — they were only talking about it.

"We did it in school for Christmas," Shea was saying. He's nine. "To make a piñata. That's made of papier-mâché. In Mexico, they make a hollow one, fill it with candy, and then hit it with a stick to break it, so that the candy comes out."

"A Halloween piñata?" asked seven-year-old Jackie.

"Yeah!" exclaimed Shea, his eyes lighting up.

"Piñatas?" I said. "I thought you were working on costumes."

"We finished our costumes," explained Jackie. "But we want something really, really special for the parade."

Okay, I should have seen it coming. Not for nothing is Jackie called the Walking Disaster. I should have known that Jackie and the newspaper strips, water, flour, and salt that are the ingredients of papier-mâché would be a volatile combination. But I was too busy being impressed by the idea.

"A Halloween piñata sounds pretty special," I said. "Good idea." (Yes, I actually said that!) "Let's go down to the kitchen and make sure we have all the supplies."

Soon we had gathered around the kitchen

table, a stack of newspapers from the recycling bin on one side, a bowl of water and flour and salt mixed into a paste on the other.

Cutting the newspaper into strips went without incident. Jackie and Shea had made piñatas before. "If we blow up a balloon, we could put papier-mâché on it . . ." Jackie frowned, thinking hard, trying to figure out how to say what he envisioned.

Shea caught on instantly. "And then pop the balloon, and stick the candy inside."

"We have balloons! Left over from birthday parties," said Jackie.

We studied the balloon collection for awhile. In the end, the long, skinny balloon won out. Why? Because the Rodowskys wanted to make a piñata that looked like their dog, Bo.

"And some little dogs. Piñata puppies," added Archie, who's four.

We had soon blown up one big balloon and three puppy ones. We began to wrap the balloons with the strips of newspaper dredged through the flour mixture. We made feet and ears of papier-mâché, too, and set them aside to dry, to be glued on when the bodies of the dog figures had dried.

"Will we be able to paint them?" asked Archie.

"Sure," I said. "Plain old tempera paint will do it. And don't forget to leave an opening on top so you can pop the balloon and take it out when everything dries, and put the candy in."

"How long do we have to wait?" asked Archie.

"Let it dry overnight," I answered.

"What if it doesn't dry in time?" asked Jackie.

"It will," I assured them. I hoped I was right.

"We could put them in the dryer," Archie offered.

"No, silly," said Shea. "If you put these in the dryer, it would tumble them around and around into pieces."

Not to mention what it would do to the inside of the dryer, I thought with a shudder.

"Let's put them up high, on a shelf in the den," I suggested. They could dry there, and they'd be safe (safe from Bo, who was eyeing these soon-to-be replicas of himself with hungry suspicion). It was while I was spreading out some newspapers, with Shea and Archie's help, that Jackie returned to the kitchen and came up with the idea of making a papier-mâché mask by molding it to his face.

I wasn't gone that long, truly I wasn't. But somehow, in that short space of time, Jackie had wound his whole head with papier-mâché strips.

It was a horrifying sight. Even Shea jumped when we walked back into the kitchen, and Jackie turned to confront us, globs of papier-mâché in one hand.

He looked like a disintegrating mummy. Strips of wet, gooey paper dangled from his head and face. Blobs of paste dripped down the front of his shirt like mummy drool. He grinned and threw his hands out. More papier-mâché paste scattered across the kitchen.

I instinctively ducked.

"I'm making a mask," said Jackie triumphantly.

"Cool," said Shea. Archie started forward, and Bo began to bark.

"Whoa. Stop. Wait a minute, Jackie."

He stood there, smiling (horribly) up at me through his papier-mâché "mask," and added, pointing, "I'm going to use the blow-dryer to make it dry faster."

How fast does papier-mâché dry? I wondered, fighting a rising sense of panic. My next thought was, thank goodness Jackie didn't plug the blow-dryer in. He could have been electrocuted.

"A blow-dryer," Shea said. "Excellent idea, Jackie."

Jackie smiled even more widely. Good grief! He even had papier-mâché on his teeth.

"Jackie," I said, "a papier-mâché mask *is* a good idea. But you can*not* use the blow-dryer, and you can't wear one until it dries. How would you get it off? And besides, it might stick to your skin and hair and that would hurt the way it does when you take off a Band-Aid."

Jackie thought about this for a minute. "Oh," he said. "I guess you are right."

"We need to wash that off," I said. "*Before* it dries."

"But what about our papier-mâché masks?" wailed Archie.

I looked around, hoping for inspiration. Fortunately, it came. "If you have any plain masks, we can decorate those with papier-mâché."

Shea's eyes brightened and Jackie gave me another papier-mâché grin.

"Come on," I said to Jackie. "Let's go get cleaned up." I warned Shea and Archie not to touch *anything*, especially the papier-mâché, and led Jackie to the bathroom.

It wasn't easy. But at last I got Jackie cleaned up.

I returned to find Shea and Archie in the kitchen. They had assembled a huge collection of Halloween masks, from what looked like every Halloween at the Rodowskys' since the beginning of time.

Shea looked up as I led his damp, scrubbed,

but still irrepressibly cheerful brother into the kitchen. He and Archie were surrounded by a huge heap of newspaper strips, through which Bo was plowing with happy whiffling sounds. "We have some more ideas for Halloween," he said. "And for new costumes. Are you ready to make our masks?"

"Just call me 'that masked man,'" I said. It was a bad joke, from the old *Lone Ranger* series on television. The Lone Ranger rides away at the end of every episode, and someone always asks, "Who was that masked man?"

No one laughed. Jackie pulled my hand and made me sit down, and Shea pushed an un-mâchéd mask toward me. "You have to *make* a mask first," he explained kindly.

Stacey

Clues, clues everywhere. I wish
I could just turn them into a
mathematical equation. Then I
could solve the mystery! But
right now, nothing adds up....

Kristy hammered on our door early the next morning. "Hurry up," she called. "I want to get downstairs early and grab a table in the corner where we can talk this case over."

When Kristy calls, we obey, at least when she has a good reason like this. Abby and I went into high speed and were soon on our way downstairs. We passed Mal at the door of the room she shared with Eileen. "Just come down when you are ready," she was saying. "Don't worry about it. I'll save you a seat at our table."

We made it to the dining room early, and secured our corner table. Mallory passed the notebook around, and we read the notes while we ordered. It was all there: my experience in the museum, the description of the scrap of inn stationery with the numbers on it, Mary Anne and Abby's discovery in the bushes, and what Mary Anne had overheard, plus detailed descriptions of each suspect.

"It strikes me," I said, "that you have a lot more notes about Martha Kempner than anyone else. Is she your main suspect, Mallory?"

Mallory's cheeks reddened. "No. Of course not."

"Descriptions of what she is wearing and everything. No one else rates that."

"She's a famous author," explained Mallory.

"So even if she isn't a suspect, everything about her is important."

"Hmmm," said Abby. "Now, if she were, say, a famous soccer player. Or basketball player —"

Kristy sternly called us to order. "Okay, let's go over this again."

We went over everything that had happened, and narrowed our list of suspects to Sean Knowles, Harvey Hapgood, Mrs. Moorehouse, Naomi Furusawa, and Martha Kempner.

"I don't know about Mrs. Moorehouse," I said. "It's just not logical. She's in a wheelchair, for one thing. I can't see her sneaking into the museum and stealing the diamond unnoticed."

"Maybe she's the mastermind behind it, and Naomi is her partner," suggested Mary Anne.

"It would make sense if she had insurance. If she doesn't, then no. And you heard her say she has no insurance. She might say that to other people to throw them off track, but she wouldn't say it to her own partner."

"But maybe Naomi isn't her partner," Abby pointed out. "It could be someone else."

"True. So we'll keep Mrs. Moorehouse's name on the list," said Mallory.

Mary Anne leaned over my shoulder and studied the notes for a moment, then observed that Sean Knowles and Harvey Hapgood might be in league for the diamond. After all, she had seen them whispering in the hall together, while no one had ever seen them even acknowledge one another publicly otherwise.

I reminded her that Sean Knowles had some kind of official credentials, and was apparently working on the case.

It was Abby, of course, who said, "Well, even if he's a cop or something, that doesn't rule out the possibility that he's after the diamond. He could just be using his job as a cover. In fact, he probably stole the diamond, hid in the museum, and just reappeared when the alarm went off. I bet he had it in his pocket when you saw him there, Stacey."

"In your dreams," Kristy blurted out.

"Happens all the time," said Abby. Everybody at the table burst out laughing at the indignant expression on her face.

When we'd stopped laughing, Mal said, "Still, it's a possibility we can't overlook."

Sean Knowles and Harvey Hapgood both remained on the list.

Martha Kempner did, too, despite Mallory's reluctance to include her. "Why would she steal the diamond?" Mallory said. "She's rich from all her books. And movies. And that series on public television, too, I bet."

"Maybe she did it for publicity," Mary Anne

said. "With the diamond stolen, she might be able to turn the article into a whole book."

"But she doesn't need to do that," Mallory insisted. "Any publisher would jump at the chance to publish anything that Martha Kempner wrote."

"Well, she may not have had a motive we can see, but she had the opportunity and the ability," said Kristy, "so we have to leave her on the list."

In the end, the only person we crossed off our list was Naomi Furusawa, and we left a question mark next to her name. We eliminated her on the basis of the wig evidence. With her long, black straight hair, why would Ms. Furusawa need to wear a wig of long, black straight hair?

"Unless she was using it as a double-blind," said Abby.

That's when Mallory put the question mark next to the nurse's crossed-off name.

At that moment, Eileen appeared at the entrance to the dining room. Mallory gestured to her to come join us and we stopped talking about the mystery.

Looking up, I realized that the dining room was nearly full, mostly with kids from SMS. Since it was a Saturday morning, I figured most of the adults (except our chaperons, of course) had probably taken the opportunity to sleep late. I also noticed that Cary Retlin and Alan Gray and a couple of other guys from the group had managed to snag a table right next to us. Alan was acting goony, as usual, but Cary was sitting with his back to us, apparently staring at his plate. I wondered if he had overheard any of our conversation. I didn't have quite the same kind of grudge against Cary that Kristy did, but I was wary of him. The less he (or anyone else, for that matter) knew of what we were doing, the better.

I turned my attention back to our table just as Eileen pulled a chair out. She was starting to sit down when Alan seemed to leap out of nowhere to yank the chair out from under her.

Mallory grabbed Eileen from one side and Mary Anne grabbed her from the other, keeping her upright.

The room fell silent. I heard what sounded like the beginning of one of Cokie's laughs, but it stopped mid-bray.

Alan stood there, holding the chair and looking foolish.

"What are you going to do for your next trick, Alan," said Kristy loudly. "Pick your nose?"

"Quit being a bully, Alan," said Mallory, almost as loudly. "You — and Cokie — and everyone — you're just like those witchhunters,

154

going after people because you can. It's not fair. It's not right. And it's stupid and ignorant."

Well, what could Alan say to that? Not much. Not after all this time spent in Salem, learning about the evils of witchhunting and persecuting innocent people for being different.

Alan looked around. Then, sheepishly, he put the chair back and returned to his table. Cokie still hadn't dared laugh or say one nasty thing.

Our confrontation with her last night and our stand against Alan this morning had stopped the witch-hunt of Eileen that had sprung up in our own class.

I hoped it would never happen again.

After that, breakfast was a pretty quiet affair. I finished quickly, knowing we had another long day of sightseeing ahead. I went up to my room, hoping to squeeze in a few minutes' work on my project before it was time to go.

I reviewed my notes and jotted down a couple of new ideas. Then I went to the closet, hunting for some comfortable shoes. I bent over to pick up my sneakers, and as I straightened up I came nose-to-combination lock with a small wall safe set into the back of the closet. Now why hadn't I noticed that before? I wondered. "A five-digit safe combination for this room is available at the front desk," read a sign pasted to the safe.

"A safe," I muttered. "A safe." The numbers on the scrap of inn stationery flashed before my eyes. Five numbers. Five numbers that could — no, *had* to be the combination to a safe somewhere in this inn!

"I have it!" I cried. "I have it!"

"The flu?" guessed Abby, who had just returned to the room. "The meaning of life?"

"No," I said triumphantly. I shoved aside coats, dresses, and hangers, and pointed to the wall safe. "Not the meaning of life. The meaning of the five numbers I found on that piece of paper in the museum."

CHAPTER 15

Kristy

Sunday

I had found a clue, too. And although it might not have been the best decision I ever made, I wanted to do some sleuthing on my own before I shared the clue with the others....

Kristy

I had just come out of my room when I saw it: a small, folded square of white paper, lying on the carpet next to Mr. Hapgood's door. For some reason, I picked it up. At the same moment, Stacey burst out of her room, proclaiming that she'd solved the numbers clue. Anyone could have heard her, including Mr. Hapgood.

"Shhh!" I hissed, pushing her back into her room. I snagged Mary Anne and Mallory and, since we were due downstairs in about one minute to join our groups for sightseeing, I called an emergency meeting of the BSC upon our return.

"Go on down," I told them. "I have to, uh, pick up my camera." Since my camera was one of those small, disposable ones, no one could tell that I already had it in my coat pocket. "I'll catch up," I added.

I hurried back to my room and closed the door. Then I smoothed out the paper on my palm and my heart started to pound. It was obviously part of a larger sheet of paper that had been ripped up. On it were the words, "must destroy the evidence in the mu —" and on the line below, "— econd floor in the north cor —" The rest of the words had been torn away.

My head began to spin. The paper must have
fallen out of Mr. Hapgood's trash container
when the cleaning staff had emptied his gar-
bage. This proved he was involved in the theft.
And that he had a partner.

I had to get to the museum before the thieves
destroyed the evidence. I didn't know what the
evidence was, but I would worry about that
later. At least I knew where it was: second
floor — which must be the room on the second
floor where the diamond had been — north corner.

But how? How could I escape the buddy system?

Sneakiness.

I told Coach Wu I was going with Mr. Baker's
group, and told Mr. Baker I was going with
Coach Wu's group. After ducking a question
from Abby, who was in Coach Wu's group, I
made myself scarce until everybody had left. I
hated to do it, because our teachers trusted us
and this was no way to repay that trust. But
with luck no one would notice the switch, and I
could slip back into the fold later without anyone being the wiser.

I told myself that there was another good reason not to tell Mary Anne or the others about
this clue. The less they knew, the less they could

tell if a teacher did start asking questions. I have to admit, though, that part of me was just dying to solve this mystery alone. I guess I was still miffed at missing so much of the action on Thursday.

The museum, of course, was still closed. Yellow crime scene tape crisscrossed the front entrance. I circled the building, trying to look inconspicuous. How *was* I going to get in? Suddenly, I saw a man in a suit, carrying a briefcase, emerge from a side door. He looked at his watch, shook his head, and hurried away.

I darted forward and grabbed the door with my fingertips just before it slammed shut.

"Ow," I said, through clenched teeth. But what are a few smashed fingers when you are about to solve a mystery? I pried the door open and slipped inside.

The door slammed behind me, and I jumped. Then I grabbed the knob.

Too late. The door was locked. My heart sank. Did this mean I was locked inside? Suddenly the museum looked big and shadowy and dark. Where were the other exits?

Forgetting, momentarily, about the clue, I walked as softly as I could down the long hall. Old-fashioned doors with frosted-glass windows, the kind with names of people and departments stenciled in black and gold script, lined the hallway. Some light shone dimly through the glass, but the doors themselves were locked.

How was I going to get out?

I walked on until I reached a large, solid door, and pushed it open.

I was in one of the exhibit rooms of the museum. As the door closed behind me, I fumbled instinctively along one wall. I flicked what felt like a switch, and a row of lights on the far wall went on. I headed for them. Glass cases glinted dimly as I passed, and I could see the sparkle of jewelry and the oblongs of white paper that labeled the collections. But I ignored these. The diamond hadn't been in this room. It had been in a room on the second floor. I reached a door in the far wall and pushed it open.

I was now in a room full of furniture, from what I could tell by the dim light. I found another set of light switches, pressed one, and lit up the replica of a ship's captain's quarters on the far wall. I spotted another door across the room. Feeling like a rat in a maze, I started toward it, weaving in and out among beds and chairs and lamps.

The lights went out when I was halfway across the room.

Kristy

I froze.

Don't panic, don't panic, don't panic, I told myself.

My heart felt as if it were going to leap out of my chest. My knees turned to jelly. My mouth was as dry as if it had been filled with sand.

Don't panic.

The door was straight ahead, remember? I told myself. It probably led to the main hall. Maybe the lights I had hit were on a timer switch. When I reached that door, I could turn on the lights in the next room.

I inched forward, paused, and considered trying to go back. But that way out was locked, and besides, what if I knocked over one of the chairs or lamps I had dodged crossing the room? I was pretty sure no major antique or valuable was directly between me and the door.

I slid my feet forward, hands out, groping.

I touched something soft.

"Urrgh," I said, before my hands discovered that what I was feeling was the back of a chair, not someone's shoulder.

Chill, I told myself. Who would be here anyway? The museum was closed, and even if Hapgood and his accomplice were headed for the scene, they hadn't arrived yet.

I hoped.

162

Patting the chair to keep my bearings, I edged around and crept forward.

And stopped again. Suddenly. So suddenly that I heard the footsteps in the dark behind me before they could stop, too.

Someone was in there with me.

I wasn't alone after all.

CHAPTER 16

MaryAnne

Sunday

The clues in the mystery
and all the things we
were learning about Salem
were getting mixed up in
my mind. By the time
we returned from sightseeing,
my head was spinning.
Little did I know just
how mixed up everything
was about to become....

"Bad pumpkin," scolded Abby, "bad pumpkin." She unclipped the pumpkin from its "leash" and held it up and waved her finger at it. "*Baaad* pumpkin."

"Poor pumpkin," Stacey said, grinning. "What has it done to deserve all that?"

Our group, the largest one, had gone for a tour of Pickering Wharf, which was as much a shopping expedition as a tour. "Like the South Street Seaport," Stacey remarked, looking around. "It's a shopping mall in a historical disguise."

"What do you mean?" I asked, as we meandered through the maze of shops and galleries and restaurants and food stands that lined the wharf.

"You know, this was once a wharf, full of ships docking to load and unload. South Street Seaport is the same. It was once one of Manhattan's working piers. Now it's full of shops." She grinned suddenly. "Of course, I do like to shop."

That was when Abby careened into us. "There you are," she said breathlessly.

"Where else would we be?" asked Mallory.

Abby shook her head. "Weird," she muttered. "One minute I was looking at the sign for the whale-watching tours, and the next minute I

165

was sort of, I don't know, pushed to one side. Then someone bumped me from the other side and I grabbed my wallet to make sure my pocket wasn't getting picked —"

"Good thinking," Stacey put in. "Sometimes, crooks work together. One distracts you and the other steals your wallet."

"I know," said Abby. "Anyway, I got all turned around, and I figured I was lost. I saw this alley and thought I'd cut through it, because I was sure you would be on the other side. And then I had the strangest feeling I was being followed."

"You didn't go down a dark alley *by yourself*," Mallory gasped.

"No! There were people around, and it wasn't really an alley. It was lined with shops. You just couldn't drive cars through it. Anyway, I looked over my shoulder, and I could have sworn that I saw someone duck back into one of the shops. So I ducked into another shop and saw you guys outside through the window."

Looking over my shoulder nervously, I said, "Followed?"

"Nah," said Abby. "I wasn't really being followed. Why would anybody do that? It was all the dastardly work of my bad-luck pumpkin."

And that's when she held it up and started to scold it.

We shopped for a little while longer, being careful not to become separated from one another or the group. Then we converged on the food stands for lunch. After that, footsore and stuffed and (some of us) burdened with packages, we headed back to the inn.

Kristy hadn't returned yet. I straightened up the room a little and flopped back on the bed, calling "come in," when Abby and Stacey and Mallory knocked on the door.

"Where's our fearless leader?" Abby asked, flopping down on the other bed.

"I guess her group hasn't come back yet," I answered.

Mallory frowned. "There are only two other groups. And Eileen's group is back, the one that Ms. Bernhardt was leading."

"Then she must be with Mr. Blake. He and Mrs. Blake took the other group," said Stacey.

"Nooo," I said slowly. "Kristy did Mr. Blake's tour already. Why would she do it again?"

"She probably stopped by the library or something," I suggested, but I felt a faint tickle of worry. I sat up. "We should check."

We checked. We checked the front desk. We checked the dining room. We checked (casually, to avoid arousing any suspicion) to see if Kristy had stopped by anybody else's room.

She hadn't. Of course she hadn't. She would

never miss a meeting of the BSC, especially an emergency meeting.

The afternoon was ticking away. Mr. and Mrs. Blake returned.

No Kristy.

Super-casually, I asked Mr. Blake if Kristy had liked the tour with him that morning. "Kristy didn't go with me today. She did that yesterday," he replied. He laughed. "I'm going to be qualified to be a tour guide before this is over."

I forced myself to smile.

"No Kristy," I reported to the others, who were hovering unobtrusively near the elevator.

"Time for an emergency meeting," said Stacey in a low voice. "Sans Kristy."

We went back up to my room. That's when Abby said, "Oh. Now I remember. Kristy said something about a clue this morning, when I asked her about going to the wharf. 'I don't need to shop for new clues,' she had said. I just thought she was making a dumb joke about shopping for clothes."

"I don't think it was a dumb joke," I said. "I mean, I think she meant something by it."

"Maybe that means she had a new clue," said Mallory.

"It has to," agreed Stacey. "But what?"

"Maybe she just figured out something that we overlooked," offered Mallory. She pulled the mystery notebook out of her briefcase and opened it. We pored over it again.

I said, slowly, "You know, you have tons of stuff in here about Martha Kempner, Mal, but the one thing you don't have is that she was the only one who didn't head for the museum when the crime was reported. Look: Ms. Furusawa, Mrs. Moorehouse, even Harvey Hapgood. Plus the newspaper spy, Sean Knowles, was right on the scene. But not Ms. Kempner. Could that be a clue?"

"Why? How?"

"Maybe because she was guilty and didn't want to return to the scene of the crime," Stacey suggested.

Abby was shaking her head. "No, no, no. The obvious thing to do would be to go to the scene of the crime with everyone else. Leave your fingerprints around and stuff like that, to cover for yourself in case you left evidence behind without realizing it."

"Ms. Kempner could be the one," I said stubbornly. "And Kristy figured it out, and then Kempner found out somehow and kidnapped her."

Mallory had picked up the room phone. "Hello, front desk? . . . Yes, is Ms. Kempner in her room? . . . No? . . . No, thanks. I'll try again later."

She hung up. "Ms. Kempner isn't in her room. She told Mr. Hewson that she was going to the newspaper office, to do some more research on the diamond."

"What about Harvey Hapgood and Sean Knowles?" asked Abby.

Abby went to her room, and Mallory went to hers, where they called to check. They returned to report that Mr. Hapgood and Mr. Knowles were gone, too, to a famous tearoom that had a fortune-teller (Mr. Knowles) and on a carriage tour of Salem (Mr. Hapgood).

"Any one of those could be a cover," Abby pointed out. "We should check their alibis."

"How . . . oh. We could call the newspaper and see if Ms. Kempner is there, or has been there," I said, my hand on the phone.

"Ditto the tearoom," said Abby, springing to her feet to rush back to her room and call.

"I guess we could call the tour company and see if anyone matching Mr. Hapgood's description was on the carriage ride," said Mal. "But those tours are kind of random. I mean, if you've made a reservation, they take your name, but you don't really have to make a reservation."

She returned to her room.

We quickly discovered that 1) no one named Martha Kempner or matching Ms. Kempner's

170

description had signed in to use the newspaper files that day; 2) Mr. Knowles had not been to the tearoom, because the tearoom closed early, so he wouldn't have had time; 3) Mr. Hapgood had called to cancel his carriage tour just before he was supposed to take it, and hadn't even complained about forfeiting his deposit.

"None of them have alibis!" cried Abby, when we met back in my room to compare notes. "Could they *all* be working together?"

"I don't know," I said, trying to keep the panic out of my voice. "But . . ." I pointed at the window. "It's getting dark, and Kristy is still missing. And in case you haven't noticed, a storm is blowing up."

We still hadn't told the adults that Kristy was missing. I was just beginning to wonder if we should when an enormous clap of thunder rattled the window — and all the lights went out.

CHAPTER 17

Shannon

You know, parades may be kid stuff, but
you never outgrow them. There is a kind
of magic to them. Not the kind of magic
that Jordan was pretending to throw
around. But then, I guess he won't be up
to those tricks anymore, at least for
awhile. Poor Jordan! He was so surprised
when he thought his magic spells were
backfiring on him!

"That's it. Homework done. At least for now," said Claudia with a sigh. She looked at the clock on her desk. "And just in the nick of time."

"Are you sure you're ready to stop? My mom could probably wait, if you need to work longer," I said.

I had stopped by Claudia's house on my way home from the library, so that my mom and I could give her a ride over to Kristy's for the parade.

"Hey, don't worry," said Claudia. "*I'm* not worried."

"Do you want me to check with my mom? We still have a little more time," I persisted.

"Like you want to sit here and watch me do homework," said Claudia. She made a face.

I shrugged. "That's what I've been doing at the library this morning."

Claudia pulled a worse face. "Well, I don't know about you, but I've had it up to here with school. Not that I don't appreciate your concern, Shannon."

"Are you getting help from your teacher?" I inquired.

"Nah. I mean, I have before. But I hate to have to keep asking. When I ask in class, everyone looks at me like I'm a goon. And when I stay after class to ask, I always feel like some dumb little kid." Claudia stood up abruptly. "Forget it. Let's go to the parade."

The Brewer-Thomases were all ready when we arrived. "This parade was a great idea," said Kristy's mom, when she let us in.

"It's a natural," agreed Nannie, who was holding what appeared to be a baby bunny in her arms: Emily Michelle, sporting long ears, with a pink nose and whiskers painted on her cheeks. A big felt carrot was sewn to her jumpsuit.

Karen was dressed as a jack-in-the-box, with a gaily painted cardboard box held on by two shoulder straps. She kept crouching down and springing up.

"I'll do this during the *whole* parade," she declared, "so people will know who I am."

"It makes my legs ache just to think about it," Claudia remarked to me.

I nodded. Kids were beginning to arrive for the parade, along with parents and their cameras of every kind. Video memories were in the offing, as well as scrapbook moments.

The Rodowskys showed up with disgusting monster masks on, carrying a collection of piñatas that roughly resembled Bo, and leading Bo himself on a leash.

"Oh, this is excellent," cried Claudia, and swooped over to greet her fellow artists.

Jessi appeared with her family. Her sister Becca was dressed as a princess, right down to glittery high heels on which she was wobbling, somewhat erratically, and clutching her father's arm. My eyes widened when I saw Squirt, Jessi's baby brother. Squirt, who is about a year and a half old, is fond of playing with pots and pans in the kitchen. Riding on his mother's shoulders and waving his hands happily, he was wearing a pot backwards on his head (made of aluminum foil, I think) and had on an apron with a potholder tied to it.

"He's coming as the king of the kitchen," explained Jessi, seeing my expression.

Logan joined us as Claudia returned. "The two Pike wagons just pulled up," he said out of the corner of his mouth, like a gangster in some old movie. "Everybody ready?"

We nodded solemnly.

Jordan and his claim to magic fame had gone too far. In fact, it had gone to his head — not the magic, but the power his pretense to magical abilities was bringing him. Not only was he claiming credit for things such as his siblings' good grades on tests (never mind how much hard work they had put into studying), but he was also warning people that if they didn't do what he told them to do, he would put spells on them. Bad spells.

For instance, when Vanessa had refused to let Jordan have her dessert at dinner. "This *spells* trouble for you," Jordan had said, giving her a warning look.

"Pooh to you," retorted Vanessa.

"Vanessa, be careful," Claire had gasped.

Vanessa had shrugged.

And then she had fallen and cut her knee and had to have a tetanus shot ("just as a precaution," her mother had insisted, despite Vanessa's vehement objections). And Jordan had said, "See? I told you so."

This time, Vanessa didn't say "Pooh."

The other kids were treating Jordan as if he were a king, and of more than just the kitchen.

He led the way toward us now. He was dressed as — what else? — Merlin the magician. His siblings followed him at a respectful distance.

"Oh. I forgot my magician's wand," said Jordan, stopping. He looked over his shoulder expectantly.

"I'll get it," cried Nicky.

"I'll help," Claire offered, and they raced back to the Pike station wagons to retrieve it. When they returned, Nicky breathlessly handed the cardboard wand (a dowel with a glitter-and-gold-coated cardboard star stapled to it) to Jordan. He took it, lowered his head like a royal prince, and didn't even say thank you!

We were stepping in just in time.

Jordan walked up to us and raised his wand. "I want to lead the parade," he announced.

"Oh, no," I said. "The youngest and smallest are going to go first."

He shook his head. "No. I should lead it."

"Why?" asked Logan.

"We've already decided how the parade is going to be organized, Jordan," said Jessi. She glanced over at us, then said, "You can't make us do everything you want, you know."

"I can," said Jordan, frowning. "And I will."

He withdrew, and turned his back on everyone. I saw him whisk his book out of one of the big pockets of his magician's cape (which was, I think, an old choir robe). A moment later he returned. We watched as he raised his wand and closed his eyes. His lips began to move.

His brothers and sisters edged away, looking from Jordan to us and back uneasily.

Then he lowered his wand. "Well," he said.

I made my face blank. I turned to Jessi. "We must make Jordan the leader of the parade," I said in a flat, wooden voice.

Jessi nodded. "Yes, we must."

Shannon

"We must," echoed Logan.

"We must," agreed Claudia.

Moving stiffly, Claudia took Jordan by the shoulder and propelled him to the front of the group of kids gathered on the lawn.

The kids were ready. People from the neighborhood were out on their lawns and on the sidewalk. The street had been temporarily blocked off (thanks to Kristy's stepdad).

"Let the First Annual Stoneybrook Halloween Costume Parade begin!" Claudia said. She motioned Jordan forward. We moved forward, too, to stand by Claudia, and signaled everyone else to stay in place.

Jordan the mighty magician strolled forward. He reached the middle of the road. He took a few more steps and turned.

"Come on," he said.

"Oh, no. You must lead the parade," chanted Claudia. "You must be out front."

Jordan frowned. He turned and took a few more steps forward, then turned again.

"Come on," he said.

"We cannot," said Jessi. "We have been ordered to let you lead the parade."

"We must obey," Logan put in.

"But . . ." Jordan frowned harder. He turned and walked several more steps. A few people applauded. A few other people laughed.

"Don't laugh at me!" shouted Jordan, raising his wand. He looked at his wand. He looked back at the rest of the kids, standing in Kristy's yard.

"I order you to start the parade," he commanded us.

"We have," I replied. "Lead on, oh mighty magician."

Jordan's face turned red. "You're supposed to do what I tell you!" he shouted.

"We are under the power of your spell," said Jessi. "We cannot disobey."

"Then I hearby change the spell," said Jordan.

"I felt no change of spell," intoned Logan. "Has the mighty magician changed the spell? Perhaps it is not in his power."

"Look in your book and have the spell unmade," called Vanessa, "so we can join in the parade."

Jordan reached into his pocket and pulled out his book. He opened it, then closed it again.

"Can't you find the right spell?" asked Byron.

His face bright red, Jordan said, "No!"

No one said anything. The great magician looked at his subjects. Then he slowly walked back toward them. He stopped in front of Jessi and Logan and Claudia and me. "It's not really a book of spells," he said in a low voice, "it's just an old book of poems. And I'm not really a magician. I just pretended."

"You didn't make me find my lucky penny?" asked Nicky.

"Or make me get a tetanus shot?" added Vanessa, looking vastly relieved.

"No. Not any of that stuff. It just happened. I can't cast spells. I just pretended, for fun."

Claire cried, "I'm not going to get to fly? You *promised*."

"I . . . it was just a joke, Claire. I didn't really . . ."

But his little sister wasn't listening. She took a deep breath. Tears welled up in her eyes. She stamped her feet, and her colorful cardboard wings flapped wildly. "Nofe air!" she howled.

It looked as if she was about to revert to an old bad habit, a full-blown temper tantrum. And I couldn't blame her. If I had believed I was going to fly and my big brother had told me it was all a "joke," I certainly wouldn't laugh.

Claudia bent over and picked Claire up and began to soothe her.

"I'm sorry," said Jordan, looking miserable. "I'm sorry, Claire. I can't make you fly, but I could carry you on my shoulders during the parade."

Claire sniffled. "Really?"

Jordan nodded. "You'll be up high in the air.

Would you like that? You can even hold my magic wand, okay?"

Claire sniffled again, then hiccuped. Then she nodded and smiled.

Byron said, "I'll help you, Jordan."

"I will, too," said Adam.

"Jordan, you have to know when to stop pretending and tell the truth," said Logan sternly. "Pretending to cast spells to get what you want isn't right."

"I know," said Jordan. "I know." He took Claire from Claudia and hoisted her to his shoulders. He handed Claire his wand.

She waved it in the air.

"Poof!" she cried. "Parade."

Claudia nodded and said once more, "Let the First Annual Stoneybrook Halloween Costume Parade begin!"

And this time, it did.

CHAPTER 18

Mallory ☺

Sunday

Okay, the inn is not haunted. I don't really believe in ghosts. But I do believe in criminals. And the kind of criminal who would steal a diamond like the Witch's Eye is not someone you want to meet by the light of day, much less by the light of a candle in a dark old New England inn.

The wind began to howl and so, I'm afraid, did we, along with most of the other people in the inn.

"It's just the storm," said Stacey. This observation was underscored by another crack of thunder immediately followed by another flash of lightning, which illuminated the whole room. I did not like the effect. It made the dark afterward seem even darker.

"Did anyone pack a flashlight?" I called out.

No one had. After all, it wasn't as if we were going camping in the woods.

Just then I heard a familiar voice in the hall. "Calm down, everyone. Calm down." A knock sounded on the door, and I groped my way toward it. Coach Wu was standing there, a flashlight in one hand, and a box of candles in the other. Around the bottom of each candle was a little cardboard disc, or skirt, to catch dripping wax, just like the ones they give you for candlelight services in church.

"This is only temporary," said Coach Wu in a voice that brooked no argument, from people or storms. "Each of you come take a candle and a book of matches. Be very, very careful. Stay in one place until the storm is over. The electricity is temporarily out because of the storm, that's all."

With that, she was gone.

I realized that with the storm and the lights out, no one had yet discovered that Kristy was missing — except us.

We waited until Coach Wu was gone and the coast was clear. Then we ventured out into the halls of the inn.

It was very dark. The candlelight made long, jumpy shadows on the walls. Since the electricity was out, the elevator wasn't working.

"Look on the bright side of the dark side," said Abby. "At least we weren't in the elevator when that lightning threw the switch."

"You know," said Stacey in a low voice, so that we instinctively drew nearer, "this would be a good time to try to get into certain rooms and check out some of the safe combinations."

"Get into the rooms how?" I asked.

"Easy," said Stacey. "These doors don't use keys, they use computer-coded cards. That means that, with the electricity out, the doors probably don't lock automatically behind you when you leave. So if someone has left his or her room since the lights went out —"

"The door isn't locked," concluded Mary Anne. "Wow."

We made a U-turn and walked to Harvey Hapgood's room. But his door was locked. Wherever he'd gone, he'd either come back and locked his door from the inside, or he hadn't come back at all.

That didn't stop Abby. She actually knocked on his door. We all gasped. And breathed a sigh of relief when he didn't answer.

"What were you going to do if he answered the door?" I asked.

"Tell him he was wanted at the front desk. He'd have had to leave his room, and we could've slipped in after he left," explained Abby. "Too bad."

We headed for the stairs and stopped again, listening to the sound of heavy breathing and heavier thumps. Then a voice said, "Careful," and another said, "Okay, okay, next step, one, two, three, now."

With only the candles to light our way, we couldn't move all that fast. We crept down the stairs and stopped at the landing. One of our theories about one of the suspects had been right: Mrs. Moorehouse could walk. But barely. She was inching down the next flight of stairs with the help of Ms. Furusawa and Mr. Hewson. As we watched, she carefully lowered one foot to the next step, then the other. Then she stopped, breathing heavily.

"Agatha," said Ms. Furusawa. "The lights will be back on in a minute and we can take the elevator. This is *too* much for you!"

Mallory

"No," said Mrs. Moorehouse harshly. "I will not sit up in my room like a trapped animal! Suppose there was a fire. How would I get out of the hotel in time then, eh? Now, help me down these stairs!"

Clearly using every ounce of her energy, Mrs. Moorehouse made it to the next step. And then the next.

We went back up to our floor.

"I guess we can eliminate Mrs. Moorehouse," I said. "No way could she flee the scene of a crime. She can walk, but just barely."

"She could still be the mastermind behind it all," said Abby, then paused. She looked down the long, dark hall. It was so quiet. So dark.

"What is it?" asked Mary Anne.

Abby cocked her head, as if listening for something. Then she said, "I don't know. I guess I'm just a little twitchy. But I have the weirdest feeling we are being . . . watched."

We all stared down the hall then, realizing how easy it would be for someone to stand in the dark, just out of the light of the candles, watching us.

Waiting for us.

"Nah," said Abby after a moment. "Just twitchy, that's all. Come on, let's go. There is the emergency exit at the other end of the hall." We made our way back down the hall, past our rooms. I couldn't help myself. I kept looking over my shoulder.

Now that Abby had mentioned it, I was sure she was right. I knew it in my bones. Someone was watching us. Someone was following us.

As it turned out, I was half right. Someone wasn't following us.

But someone *was* watching us.

He stepped out of the shadows and in front of us just as we reached the exit door.

Sean Knowles.

CHAPTER 19

Kristy

                                 Sunday

Frozen spaghetti down my back makes me shriek. But this was way too serious for screaming.

I jammed my fist up against my mouth. It kept me from screaming. It kept me from running, even though my brain *was* screaming: run, run, *run!*

My foot touched something small and solid and I stooped and ran my hands over what felt like a footstool. A plan — not much of a plan, but a plan — squeezed itself in around my screaming thoughts.

Further groping brought me to a chair.

I moved the footstool out to where I had been standing. I edged around the chair.

I backed up slowly until I touched something else:

A bed. I remembered a book I'd read about someone hiding in a bed. Was it *The Mixed Up Files* of . . . no, no time to think about that now. I leaned forward, gave the chair a tremendous shove, and in the cover of the noise, made a dive over the foot of the bed.

It was an old-fashioned featherbed, and I sank into it like a stone into a pool of water, yanking covers over my head. No one would think to look for me *in* the bed in the museum, would they?

I heard the footsteps shuffle forward again. Someone was breathing heavily, as if through his nose. Good. A clue to identification, I thought, and was pleased that I was back in my Agatha Kristy mode in spite of my pounding heart.

The shuffling came closer. Closer. Something bumped against something else and a voice said, "Oww," and then stopped abruptly.

I drew my brows together. Cautiously, I lowered the covers and peered out into the darkness, straining to see.

When the person lit the match, the light was so bright, I blinked.

But that wasn't all that made me blink.

With a banshee yell, I leaped from the bed.

"Alan, you are dead!"

Alan Gray screamed like I had never heard him or any human being scream before. He didn't leap into the air, he levitated. The match inscribed an arc in the darkness and went out.

In spite of the terror I had just been through, the moment was sweet. I couldn't help myself. I began to laugh.

"W-who, w-who . . ." I heard Alan stammering.

I laughed harder. I gasped for air and leaned weakly against the bed, giddy with relief and laughter.

Alan lit another match and held it up. "K-Kristy?"

"You shouldn't play with matches," I said, and went off into another storm of laughter.

"Kristy Thomas?" said Alan.

I got a grip. "Who did you think it was? You're the one who lured me here in the first place with that bogus clue."

"Clue?" Alan looked puzzled, then said, "Oww!" and shook the match out. He lit another and looked around. A table stood nearby with a candlestick on it, and there was a candle in it.

Alan grabbed the candle and lit it.

I hoped the candle wasn't some kind of antique, but I didn't say anything. My thoughts were now darkening like a storm cloud. Why had Alan sounded so puzzled? Why had he been so, well, surprised to see me?

"What clue?" asked Alan, returning with the candle.

"What are you doing here?" I asked, and then, suddenly remembered I was in a museum, which is sort of like a library, so you're not supposed to talk loudly, *plus* I wasn't even supposed to be there. I lowered my voice to a whisper. "Didn't you set me up to scare me?"

Alan lowered his own voice to match mine. "No! You scared me! Are you the one who left the note saying I could solve the mystery of the

Witch's Eye if I came to the museum this afternoon?"

"No!" I paused. At least my clue had been more subtle. I would never have fallen for such a clearly artificial lure. But then, subtlety has never been one of Alan's strengths.

But it was definitely the strong suit of someone else who liked to play jokes. Someone who had been egging Alan on. Someone with whom I had engaged in a battle of wits before, more than once.

"Cary Retlin," I hissed.

Alan looked around.

"No, not here. At least, I hope not. Alan, this is all Cary's doing, don't you see? He lured us in here, and I bet he was going to scare us both out of our wits."

"Well, it worked," said Alan glumly.

It had worked for me, too, but I wasn't about to admit it to Alan. "How did you get in?" I demanded. "Can we get back out that way?"

"The side door was unlocked," said Alan. "But then it locked behind me."

I suddenly remembered Cary's ability to fiddle with locks. I wondered what he had done to make that door open so easily from the outside, and then lock so securely from the other side. Then I realized how smug I felt about sneaking in as the museum employee was leaving and realized that I hadn't had to be so sneaky at all. Thanks to Cary, the door was probably unlocked the whole time.

"Listen, there has to be another way out," I said. "Even if it's one of those exit doors with the alarm." I paused. "Although I think we should avoid that if we can."

Alan nodded vigorously. We headed for the far door.

The museum looked much bigger by candlelight than in the ordinary light of day. And much bigger on the inside than it looked on the outside. I don't know why that was true, but it was.

We did find one exit, lit by a bright red EXIT sign. It also had a warning on the door: Emergency Exit Only. Alarm Will Sound.

Was I ready for that? I was not.

I realized that finding Cary, who was bound to show up sooner or later, and forcing him to unlock a door that wasn't alarmed was the only way out.

That was when I came up with plan number two. We would not only force Cary to free us, we would scare him to the middle of next week. It was the least we could do to repay him.

"Alan," I hissed, pulling him to one side. "Listen. I've got an idea."

* * *

"Aaaaaah!" Alan screamed. He screamed pretty convincingly. I almost believed him. Except that I had heard him scream for real not that long before. This time, I knew it was an act. I was using Alan as bait to catch Cary.

Alan stammered (also very convincingly), "Who-who . . ."

I had to hand it to Alan. He wasn't stupid. In some cases, he learned from his experiences.

"Cary!" he gasped. *"Cary Retlin?"*

Alan must have found Cary, who laughed triumphantly. Ha, ha, to you, too, Cary Retlin, I thought, as I listened to Alan's questions and Cary's explanations from my hiding place in the next room.

I ground my teeth and thought of revenge.

Alan said loudly, so I could hear from where I was waiting, "You have one of those little flashlights. I wish I had one."

"It's a keychain light," said Cary. "So you want to help me scare Kristy?"

"Sure . . . when?"

"Any minute now." Cary lowered his voice. "She'll be up in the room where the diamond was on display. We'd better head up there."

"But Kristy is baby-sitting for Ms. Garcia," said Alan.

"No, she's not," said Cary. "That's Mary Anne."

Interesting, I thought. Cary clearly kept us all under close surveillance.

"I don't know about that. But Mary Anne hadn't been on one of the tours she needed for her project and Kristy had, so Ms. Garcia asked Kristy . . ." Alan's voice trailed off. "Maybe that's why Kristy tried so hard to weasel out of it!"

"But she didn't?" asked Cary.

"Nope. She went with Nidia and a couple of other kids and Mrs. Bernhardt to the wax museum to make tomb rubbings. As they left the inn, Kristy was explaining how they couldn't make tomb rubbings of real tombs because that would wear away the stone just like the wind and the rain did."

I grinned appreciatively at that. It was a nice touch.

And Cary fell for it.

"Bummer," he said. "I guess we could wait, but —"

"Yeah, let's do that!" said Alan. "What's the plan? We jump out and say boo?"

"Sort of. But we can't wait around here *all* afternoon. For one thing, we'll be missed. And for another, it's already getting late."

"Everyone thinks I'm with someone else," said Alan proudly. "They won't miss me for hours."

Under normal circumstances, I would have said at that point that no one would miss Alan, ever. But I was experiencing a moment of chagrin that he and I had used the same ruse to slip away. Was it such a common one? If so, why had the chaperons fallen for it?

Did they actually trust Alan as much as they trusted *me*? It was a very lowering thought.

"No," said Cary. "Come on. Even the best laid plans of mice and ratmen sometimes go awry. Or something like that."

"You know how to get out?" asked Alan. Then he added, his voice apprehensive, "Without setting off any alarms?"

"Yup."

They walked quickly across the hall. Then Alan stopped.

"Did you hear that?" he asked.

"Hear what?"

Alan listened a moment longer, then said, "I don't know. I guess I'm just jumpy."

They opened a door. Alan said, "Cary?"

Cary had stopped, too, his head cocked.

Then Alan laughed nervously. "You don't think Kristy like, you know, brought Ms. Garcia's kid here, do you?"

"No. No way," said Cary. "Kristy is a totally responsible baby-sitter. She'd never expose any kid she was in charge of to any kind of danger."

I almost forgave Cary. Almost.

Cary muttered, "I hope it's not some guard coming on duty or something. It shouldn't be, according to my information. The police were supposed to keep this place closed all day."

"This museum isn't, um, haunted, is it?" asked Alan.

"No. Not unless you believe in ghosts," Cary replied cryptically. But he sounded unsure of himself. Even a little — afraid?

"I don't like this," said Alan. "Let's get out of here. Can't you go any faster?"

"I'm going. I'm going." Cary's hand closed on the door handle. He turned it.

It didn't open. I was holding it from the other side. I had wedged myself against the door, and a sturdy chair beneath the knob (not one of the antiques, but the guard's chair that stood next to the door).

"It won't open," Cary said.

"Let me try." Alan tried. Noisily. Dramatically. But not very hard.

Cary squatted and examined the knob. "It's not locked," he said.

"It must be stuck, then."

Alan tried again.

Then Cary did.

Alan said, on a nice note of rising panic, "We have to get out of here! Is there any other way out?"

I held my breath, but Cary answered, to my relief, "I've only got that one door rigged. All the others would set off the alarm."

Alan hurled himself at the door again. And again.

"Hey, Alan, calm down," said Cary. But he didn't sound so calm himself.

"Got to get out, got to get out," Alan panted. "What are we going to do?" His voice rose hysterically.

"I don't know," said Cary, sounding thoroughly rattled.

"Is there a phone anywhere? We could call for help!"

"If we do that, we might as well just set off one of the alarms," said Cary, sounding more and more uncertain.

It was wonderful.

Then Alan said, "Okay, if we both hit the door with our shoulders . . ."

That was my cue. As they backed up and Alan began to count (loudly) to three, I whisked the chair off to the side of the door, stepped up on it, and raised the cover from the bed high.

The door flew open, the guys sprawled out

into the room, and I dropped the cover over them. Alan began to scream hysterically and Cary's nerve broke.

He began to scream, too.

Alan crawled out from under the cover and came to stand next to me. We watched Cary scream and writhe below.

As his screams died down and he began to fight his way free, I said, in as deep a voice as I could produce from behind my hand, "You are under arrest. Please keep your hands in sight. We have you covered."

Cary's hands came out from under the cover. "But I can explain everything. It's all a mistake. I . . . I . . . I . . ." His voice trailed off as he emerged, and looked up to see Alan and me illuminated by the light of the candle that I had just relit.

We all went laugh ballistic. Even Cary.

When I could manage to speak again, I straightened up and wiped my eyes. I made my voice deep and put my hand over my mouth and said, "Gotcha, Cary Retlin."

Stacey

Sunday

You'd scream, too, wouldn't you?
Sometimes, it is the only logical
thing to do.

We screamed. We screamed our heads off. We backed up so fast that most of the candles went out, leaving us in near darkness. Which made us scream even more.

Have you ever noticed how screaming is contagious?

I heard Mr. Hewson's voice from the far stairs calling, "What is it? What's going on?"

Then Sean Knowles switched on his flashlight and answered, "It's me, Sean Knowles. I just startled some of the students, that's all."

He sounded so ordinary that we stopped screaming and stood there with our mouths open.

Doors were opening along the hall, and candles were popping out into it. Mr. Knowles stepped back through the exit door and we herded right after him.

"What are you doing?" demanded Abby crossly. "You shouldn't go sneaking around like that. You could scare a person to death."

"I'm sorry," said Mr. Knowles. "You scared me, too, you know."

His face was rather ashen, I noticed. Even taking the bad lighting into account.

"Who are you, anyway?" I blurted out. "And why are you sneaking around this inn? And how come you were *right* there when the

Witch's Eye was stolen?" Being scared out of my wits had given me a kind of courage.

Mallory added, "Yes, and why are you always spying on people, like Mrs. Moorehouse?"

To our collective surprise, Mr. Knowles smiled. "I didn't know I was being so closely observed," he said. "I'll have to be more careful in the future."

He reached into his breast pocket.

"He has a gun!" shrieked Abby.

"No!" said Mr. Knowles. "I have identification."

Looking sheepish, Abby said, "When people reach into their pockets like that, in situations like this, they *could* have a gun. Happens all the time."

"Abby!" scolded Mary Anne. She smiled at Mr. Knowles — good old Mary Anne — and took the plastic i.d. case he held out. We all read it:

Sean Colvin Knowles, UltraInsurance Agency, Licensed Investigator, I.D. # 69832-1-007.

"Double-oh-seven?" gasped Mallory.

Mr. Knowles smiled again. "Just a coincidence. It's not what you think."

"So you're investigating the theft of the diamond?" asked Abby.

"I'm not at liberty to discuss the details of my client's affairs," Mr. Knowles said.

"You won't talk, eh?" asked Abby.

"Abby!" I said. "Cut it out."

Mr. Knowles actually laughed. "Nope. I won't talk. And, if you'll excuse me, I have work to do." He bounded down the stairs and turned on the landing just below. "My advice to you is to quit wandering around in this inn in the dark. You could get hurt. I can't talk about my client's affairs, but I can tell you this: There is a pretty desperate criminal on the loose, more desperate than you realize."

Then he was gone on noiseless, sneakered feet.

Abby gasped. "Do you think that was a threat?"

"Could be," I said. "A not-very-thinly-veiled one, either."

"I don't believe it. He has a nice smile," Mary Anne countered.

Mallory had sat down on the steps and was staring in the direction in which Mr. Knowles had disappeared. She appeared to be thinking hard.

"Mr. Knowles," she mused in a faraway voice. "What is it about Mr. Knowles?"

"Mal?" said Mary Anne. "Are you all right?"

"Shhh," I said.

"Mr. Knowles. Mr. Knowles bounded away on little cat feet. Noiseless, sneakered feet," Mallory went on.

Sneakered feet? I thought.

"That's it!" Mallory exclaimed.

"That's what?" I asked.

"Remember how you kidded me about writing so much about Martha Kempner, because I even wrote descriptions of what she was wearing? Well, the morning of the theft, when we saw Ms. Kempner at breakfast, she was shorter than usual. I wrote that down, too. Shorter, because she was wearing sneakers with her suit, not her usual heels. It's the only time we've seen her when she hasn't been wearing her heels."

"Everyone makes fashion mistakes," I said consolingly. "Actually, I think her stiletto heels are a bigger fashion bomb. The sneakers are an improvement. Not much of one, but an improvement."

"No. I mean, that's not the point!"

"You're right," said Mary Anne. "I remember her running out of the lobby. Why would Martha Kempner wear sneakers on the morning of the robbery?"

"To move fast — and quietly," Abby concluded.

Mal nodded and pointed down the stairs in

the direction that Sean Knowles, insurance investigator, had gone. "Just like Mr. Knowles."

"Whoa!" said Abby. "Excellent deduction, Mallory. Or do I mean induction?"

Suddenly Mallory's elation was wiped off her face by a look of guilt. "Oh, no! Not Martha!"

"Well, maybe you are wrong," said Abby. "But I hope you aren't."

"I hope I am," Mallory murmured.

I said, "Well, right or wrong, the logical thing to do, then, is to check Ms. Kempner's room safe. Do we know which room she's in?"

"I do," said Mallory with a guilty look, and led the way down to the next floor and to the author's room.

The door was open. The room was empty. In the closet were rows of neatly organized clothes. On the floor were rows of high-heeled shoes. Even the bedroom slippers had heels on them.

There was no sign of the sneakers, I noticed.

But Abby was pushing aside the clothes and saying, "What was that combination again?" so I closed my eyes and reeled it off from memory. Great. It was probably stuck in my mind for all time, along with Sean Knowles' i.d. number.

The safe (which was not, fortunately, on an electrical system) opened. There was definitely a link between the theft and Martha Kempner. The diamond wasn't there, but maybe it had been moved.

"I'll go get the notebook," Mallory said, as if she couldn't get away from the evidence fast enough.

"I think we'd better find Martha Kempner," I said. "If she is planning to escape, at least there will be three of us to try and stop her. Or we can follow her."

"Or just keep an eye on her," suggested Mary Anne. "But maybe she has already tried to get away."

"I don't think so," said Abby. "All her clothes and stuff are still here in her room."

We split up, after closing the safe and trying to make everything look as if we hadn't been there at all. Our candles were burning low. Mallory took the longest one, and the rest of us put out all but one to conserve candlepower.

When we reached our floor, we found a sign next to the door informing us that only doors on certain floors opened automatically from the stairwell.

That meant, I supposed, that they weren't on the same electrical system as the room door locks.

We trudged up another flight of stairs. The

exit door was on the opposite side there, and we found ourselves in a different wing of the inn. And then, suddenly, somehow, we were lost.

The candle burned lower and lower. We went down a flight of stairs and found ourselves on a floor with no guests. It looked as if it were being renovated. The ribs of ghostly ladders loomed up from the darkness. White dropcloths gave hall furniture ghostly shapes.

"Look," said Abby. "There's another door up there. Maybe it leads somewhere." She darted ahead.

I heard the door open. I had a sudden premonition. Something bad was about to happen.

"Abby, wait!" I called. I lurched forward after her — and the candle blew out.

"Stacey! Stacey!" cried Mary Anne, her voice rising.

"I'm right here," I said.

"Where? Keep talking."

"Right here. Right —"

A hand smacked my ribs and then clutched my sleeve. "Stacey?"

"Mary Anne?"

We established that we were in fact who we said we were. Then Mary Anne said, "We'd better light the candle again."

"Okay. Give me the matches."

"I don't have the matches."

"Well, I don't either. . . . Oh, right. Abby does."

"Then we'd better find her," said Mary Anne. She sounded calmer. Meanwhile, my pulse was beginning to race uncomfortably fast. Why did I have such a terrible feeling about this?

"Abby!" I called. "Abby!"

Something thumped. Something bumped. Something crashed.

And then Abby answered us.

With a horrible, strangled cry.

CHAPTER 21

Abby

Sunday

Never open a door and go through into the dark without a) a flashlight, or at least a working candle (why oh why had we given the extra candles to Mary Anne?) and b) a clear idea of how to find your way back to where you came from.

Abby

The door closed behind me and my momentum carried me forward, until I bumped into something hard.

"Owww," I said indignantly.

Since nobody else said "ow" or apologized, I assumed it was an inanimate object. It was. It was a wall. And my rebound had thumped me against another wall. I was completely turned around.

I put my hands out and began to grope along in the complete darkness. The wall turned. I stopped.

I had the strangest sensation — strange, but not unfamiliar — that I was being followed.

Who could follow me in the complete darkness? I thought. Naturally I came up with an answer, or rather, several answers: Vampires. Werewolves. Ghosts.

Did ghosts make scraping sounds like the one I had just heard ahead?

Weren't they more apt to moan and materialize in a shimmer of ghostly white?

Lest my pert patter make you think I wasn't scared, I was. I was now frightened out of my mind. I was just talking to myself, to keep myself from thinking.

I've noticed it works for some other people. Why shouldn't it work for me?

210

Then I remembered Sean Knowles' words. "A pretty desperate criminal is on the loose. More desperate than you realize."

That would be Martha Kempner, wouldn't it? Was I afraid of her?

No, I told myself firmly.

But what if she had an accomplice? A big, mean accomplice? A big, mean, armed accomplice? Or what if she was a small, mean, black belt in judo or karate? And armed herself?

Don't think that all this time I was standing there in the dark debating these questions. I was not. I had sense enough to keep moving.

And I knew I heard someone else moving around in the dark near me.

I toyed, momentarily, with the idea of calling for help. But what if Stacey and Mary Anne came running and whoever — or whatever — caught them? Suppose someone got hurt? Suppose I gave my position away, and whoever it was got to me first?

Maybe I could reason with the person. Happened all the time on those cop shows.

Somehow, I didn't think it happened all the time in real life. Besides, I wasn't feeling very reasonable. Terror and reason just do not mix.

I reached down and touched my pet pumpkin, which was clipped by its leash to my belt loop. "Hey, fella," I said to it (in my mind). "Don't fail me. Be a good-luck pumpkin now."

The pumpkin heard me. At least about the luck part. I still haven't decided whether it was good luck or bad.

A light flashed into my eyes, blinding me. And someone leaped from the darkness.

I struck out, and the flashlight flew away, thudding against a wall. Hands grabbed my shirt and spun me around. I balled up my fists and jabbed out hard.

Someone went "oof" and his grip on me loosened momentarily. The flashlight rolled, and the beam lit me up like I was the solo act on a stage. I scrabbled sideways, trying to get out of the beam, then thought better of it and leaped for the light.

At the same time, the person leaped for me. I flung up my hands and felt something tug at my waist. I reached down just as my pumpkin was torn loose and dropped to the floor.

It bounced once, and cracked open. Something spilled out. The person lunged across the beam of the flashlight for it and I saw . . .

Martha Kempner.

And what had to be the Witch's Eye.

In one smooth soccer move, I dribbled the diamond to one side. Then I shoved my knee into the side of Martha Kempner's knee and she gave a choked, almost gagging sound, like someone in pain. She staggered sideways. If a ref had seen me, I would have been given a yellow card for a wicked foul.

Not that I cared. I grabbed the diamond and the flashlight and turned the flashlight off. Then I turned to run, blundering into walls and who knew what else. Something went over with a crash.

Out of nowhere, another beam of light pinned me.

"Harvey, be careful," I heard Martha Kempner say from somewhere on the floor behind me. Then she moaned.

"I will," said Harvey Hapgood. He stepped forward. "Hand it over," he said.

I threw up my hands and I heard a gasp of pure horror behind me. Harvey Hapgood stopped in his tracks. Even in the faint light, I could see his face turning a funny color.

And then I saw why.

It was the Witch's Eye, with special effects added.

Dimly, I heard someone call my name. That was when I screamed for the first time. Only it came out as a strangled cry.

The diamond was glowing an eerie, horrible green.

CHAPTER 22

MaryAnne

Sunday.

It was haunted.
Cursed. And weird. I
don't care what anyone
says, there is no
logical explanation for
the way that diamond
was glowing. Wait till
I tell Dawn.

Stacey and I ran toward the sound of Abby's scream. Behind us, something crashed in the darkness. I heard a voice, which I later realized was Sean Knowles', shout, "This way! Over here!"

Footsteps pounded up the stairs. Mallory was shouting our names.

Somehow I reached the door through which Abby had gone and threw it open myself. Stacey and I charged through it — and stopped.

Not in fear. That's something else I remember now. I wasn't afraid. Everything happened too fast to be afraid.

No, we stopped in shock. Amazement. Disbelief.

Abby was a little way down the hall, turned sideways to us, her back against a wall. Harvey Hapgood was standing across the hall from her, holding a flashlight trained on her. Lying on the floor, clutching her knee and breathing in short, painful gasps, was Martha Kempner.

In Abby's hand, something glowed with an eerie green light.

As we watched, Abby took a step forward. "Stand back," she said. "Or I won't be responsible for what happens."

"The Witch's Eye," breathed Stacey. "It has to be."

215

My eyes widened. How had Abby gotten her hands on the Witch's Eye? Had she taken it away from Ms. Kempner?

"It can't be true. It's not true," gasped Martha Kempner.

"Stand back. The curse will fall on you," Abby intoned.

"There is no curse, Harvey! Don't listen to her!" Ms. Kempner cried.

Harvey Hapgood seemed to waver. He took a step forward and stopped. Abby threw back her shoulders. She brandished the diamond. "You want this cursed diamond?" she said, lowering her voice. "It brings death and destruction to whoever owns it."

"No, it does not!" Ms. Kempner shouted. "Harvey, grab the diamond and let's get out of here."

Hapgood shook his head as if to clear it. Then he took another step toward Abby, a big, menacing step. Abby's fingers closed tightly around the diamond and she tensed.

"No!" I heard myself shout and all three of them jumped.

And at that moment, the lights went on and a mass of people surged through the door behind us.

"Freeze!" someone shouted. "Police."

Harvey turned to run. Abby did something

216

weird (she told me later it was a soccer move called a slide tackle) and Hapgood stumbled forward.

Sean Knowles seemed to fly out of nowhere and land on top of Hapgood. They both went down with a floor-shaking crash.

Abby curled herself into a little ball and rolled sideways as more people filled the hallway. Someone bent over Martha Kempner. "Oww," I heard her moan. "My knee."

We headed for Abby and bent to help her up.

Mallory said in my ear, "It *was* Martha. And Harvey Hapgood, wasn't it?"

"Yes," I said. "Abby, are you all right?"

Abby uncurled and stood up. She grinned. "That was excellent, wasn't it?'

"Excellent! You call that excellent?" I seldom raise my voice. Now seemed a good time.

"Well, it *was* a little scary for awhile."

"The diamond," breathed Stacey. "I saw it. It was *glowing*."

"The diamond? You have the diamond?" gasped Mallory.

Abby held out her tightly closed fist. Slowly, dramatically, one finger at a time, she opened her hand.

We all gasped. A large, many-faceted stone with an icy, faintly golden tinge lay in the palm of her hand.

"The Witch's Eye," said Mallory.

"Yup," said Abby.

"But how? Where? Did you take it away from Martha?" Mallory asked.

"Nope. I had it all along." Abby was clearly enjoying herself hugely.

I put my hands on my hips. "Cut it out, Abby, and tell us what happened."

Abby pointed to the floor. We saw the remains of her pet pumpkin. "It was hidden in there the whole time. I'm not quite sure what happened, but Ms. Kempner must have hidden it in there. She was in the gift shop, too, remember, that morning after the robbery. She must have stashed it in the pumpkin. And then, before she could go back for it, I bought it."

"Someone *has* been following you, then," said Stacey. "It's all starting to make sense, now."

We had been so absorbed in what was going on that we hadn't even noticed the chaos around us. But now Harvey Hapgood was being led past, struggling. "It wasn't my idea," he shouted. "It was hers. She planned the whole thing!"

"Harvey, shut up, you idiot. Don't talk," Martha Kempner was shouting at him. Then she said, "I demand a lawyer. I'm going to sue. I have rights."

"Yes, you do," said a detective's voice. It was

Detective Frizell. He wasn't joking. As two other officers lifted Martha Kempner to her feet, he began to recite, "You have the right to remain silent. Anything you say can and will be used against you . . ."

Sean Knowles interrupted, "Where's the diamond, Ms. Kempner?"

They were at the door now. Detective Frizell finished reciting Ms. Kempner's rights, but she ignored him. She glared past Mr. Knowles in our direction. "Ask the brat pack over there," she snapped. "Ask the little monster who broke my leg."

"I didn't break your leg," Abby shot back, firing up. "And you started it."

For one ludicrous moment, I thought both Abby and Martha Kempner were going to stick their tongues out at each other. Then the door opened and Martha Kempner, surrounded by police officers, disappeared from sight.

Sean Knowles walked slowly over to us.

"Well?" he said.

Abby held out her hand and began her story all over again.

And at that moment, Kristy burst through the door. Her accusing gaze swept the scene. Then she charged toward us.

"Kristy! Where have you been?" I cried. "We've been worried sick about you!"

Mary Anne

"And how did you find us?" asked Stacey.

"Never mind that," said Kristy impatiently. She saw the diamond still resting on Abby's hand and she folded her arms and narrowed her eyes. "I knew it! I knew this was going to be a bad weekend! Tell me you didn't do this to me. Tell me you didn't go and solve the mystery without me!"

Kristy

Sunday

I've almost forgiven you guys. Almost. After all, the mystery did get solved and it wasn't as if I didn't help. And revenge is sweet, sweet, sweet. I don't think Cary has recovered yet.

Kristy

The storm was over, the lights were on, and it wasn't so late after all. In fact, it was still dinnertime.

After telling Sean Knowles our story, handing the diamond over to a police officer who'd remained behind, and assuring him that we'd be around to make statements, we headed for the dining room to chow down. In the lobby, we passed Detective Frizell talking to Mrs. Moorehouse and Ms. Furusawa. Mrs. Moorehouse gave us a surprised look as we went by.

I smiled.

Everything tasted great, although I couldn't tell you what we ate. We were busy talking.

We spent the rest of Halloween quietly. Mary Anne and Ms. Garcia took Nidia on a trick-or-treat excursion around the block and returned to report that the streets were even more full of weird and wonderful costumes than on the night of the parade. We helped hand out candy to the trick-or-treaters who came to the inn. And one by one, we followed Detective Frizell into Mr. Hewson's office to tell our side of what had happened.

And then suddenly, Halloween was almost over. The chaperons were lingering over coffee in the dining room. Most of our class had drifted off to bed, including Cary Retlin, who wouldn't quite look in my direction, and Alan Gray, who kept winking at me. Cokie and Grace were nowhere to be seen, but I saw Eileen head up the stairs chatting happily with another sixth-grader.

I flopped back on the sofa in the lobby. "This has been an awesome day," I said.

"You can say that again," said Abby. "But don't."

I grinned. "Did I tell you how loudly Cary screamed?"

"You did," replied Stacey. "And that part you *can* tell us again."

I was willing to oblige, but at that moment, the front door opened and Ms. Furusawa pushed Mrs. Moorehouse through. Mrs. Moorehouse had a large white box on her lap.

"There you are," said Mrs. Moorehouse. "Good. Come with us."

Puzzled, we followed them into the dining room. Mrs. Moorehouse led the way to a large round table and indicated we should sit down. A waitress appeared, as if by prearranged signal. Smiling, she began to set out plates and forks and napkins, as Mrs. Moorehouse set the box on the table, opened it, and lifted out an enormous, beautiful cake — shaped like a pumpkin!

"A local specialty," she informed us. "Fortunately, the bakery is open late on Halloween."

"Wow," said Abby. "That's one of the best-looking pumpkins I've ever seen."

Both Mrs. Moorehouse and Ms. Furusawa smiled. Then they began to put the slices on the plates. I saw that the cake had been presliced, and a moment later I saw why.

Inside each slice was a tiny gold pumpkin charm.

"A new pet pumpkin," exclaimed Abby.

"Cool," said Stacey.

Mary Anne held hers up wonderingly. "For us?"

I saw Mallory grin.

"Yes," said Mrs. Moorehouse. "To help you remember your adventure and your heroic deeds."

Mallory started turning bright red. Even I felt a little embarrassed.

Not Abby. "No problem," she said. "Happens all the time."

"Abby!" I said.

"Well, it does. We have a mystery notebook to prove it, don't we, Mallory?"

Mallory blushed more.

"Will you keep the Witch's Eye?" asked Mary Anne, tactfully changing the subject somewhat. "And will you tell us the real story of it?"

"Well, it does have a bit of a curse on it, but nothing like what Ms. Kempner told you. She's the one who planted those rumors. She had become obsessed with it."

"For real?" I said. "I mean, things like that happen in real life?"

Mrs. Moorehouse nodded. "In this instance, yes. She originally offered to buy it from me, and I declined. She pretended she was joking, and I thought no more of it. Then I started getting all kinds of offers for it. Harvey Hapgood was only the most recent."

"And the most persistent," added Ms. Furusawa.

"Meanwhile, my insurance agent had called me and told me that they could no longer insure the diamond, because of the rumors. As it turns out, that was a phony call. It was Harvey Hapgood pretending to be my agent. The diamond has been insured all along. He and Martha Kempner were just trying to add to the pressure for me to sell it. And finally, when Martha realized I didn't want to part with the diamond, she decided to resort to desperate measures."

"She disguised herself as a maintenance worker, didn't she? To get into the museum early in the morning?"

Ms. Furusawa nodded in answer to that. "She wanted to steal the diamond from the museum, because she was afraid that if she stole it directly from Mrs. Moorehouse, it would be too easy to trace back to her.

"The theft took longer than she thought and as a result was discovered more quickly. She was headed back to the inn when she was forced to duck into the bushes to avoid being seen. She took off the maintenance outfit and hid it there, intending to retrieve it later. Then she walked up the front steps. She had tucked the diamond into the small hollow ceramic pumpkin, which she had bought at another gift shop. Having already chipped a small piece out of the bottom, she put the diamond inside, and then glued it back together."

"That's why the sales clerk didn't recognize it!" exclaimed Abby. She suddenly laughed. "And she sold it to me for two dollars, because I showed her the crack in the bottom."

"Yes. Ms. Kempner was trying to act as if nothing had happened, so she went into the dining room for breakfast. When she came out again, the lobby was full of police, and she realized that she'd had her second stroke of bad luck. Mary Anne had found the disguise in the bushes, and now everybody in the inn was a potential suspect. She panicked and dropped the pumpkin off at the gift shop, intending to pick it up later."

"And Abby bought it," said Mallory. "Oh, it's all beginning to make sense now. Abby's waist pack was snatched at the parade because Ms. Kempner thought the pumpkin was in there. And when it wasn't, she used Abby's key card to get in the room and search for it."

"And you had it all along as part of your outfit," I said to Mal.

"And I *was* being followed," said Abby. "I bet they even tried to separate me from you guys down at the Wharf."

"Probably," agreed Mrs. Moorehouse.

"But what about Mr. Knowles?" asked Stacey.

"He's an insurance claims investigator. The company sent him down to keep an eye on the diamond. After all, I had it insured for quite a bit of money. And they suspected all those rumors they were hearing about the diamond's curse were a cover for me to steal the diamond and claim the money."

"If the diamond isn't a bad-luck diamond, how did it glow like that?" asked Mary Anne.

"It was just a trick of the light," said Abby.

Mary Anne shook her head. "I'm not so sure," she said.

"Whatever," said Stacey. "It kept Hapgood at bay long enough for you to be rescued."

"Or for Hapgood and Kempner to be rescued from Abby," I said slyly.

Kristy

We all laughed.

And then, suddenly, unable to stop myself, I yawned hugely. "Oh! Sorry," I said.

We headed up to bed shortly after that.

As we left, Mrs. Moorehouse called out after us, "Thank you again. And happy Halloween!"

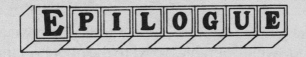

Abby

Just another ordinary meeting of the BSC — with a few extra-ordinary events to discuss. Whew. Hanging around with these baby-sitters can be a hazard to your health, especially if you are a crook!

Abby

The photos of the Stoneybrook Halloween parade were adorable. So were the photos of the Salem parade. We decided to put them in a photo album together.

Will that lead to an official BSC photo album? Hmmm. No one has said anything about it yet. Maybe I'll bring it up when we have a dull moment.

Not that it looks as though that will happen anytime soon.

"So you cured Jordan of magicianitis," said Mallory to Claudia, Jessi, Shannon, and Logan. "Good work."

"No problem," said Logan. "All in a day's work for a baby-sitter."

"Yeah, right," I said. "Like solving a major robbery. You know, little things like that."

"What a totally awesome trip," declared Claudia. "A much better learning experience than doing homework." She scooped up a handful of pretzels and an Oreo cookie, and took alternating bites.

"Yeah, but we still have to write up our projects. And we didn't get our pictures in the paper," Kristy pointed out. "You guys did."

This was true. The Stoneybrook newspaper had carried a photograph of the parade in which the Rodowskys, including Bo and the dog piñatas, were prominently featured.

"Yup. Good public relations for the club, too," Shannon added.

"Maybe we should have business cards made up," Stacey suggested. "With our club name, hours of operation, phone number."

"Not a bad idea," said Kristy.

"Yeah," I said. "I can see it now: the Baby-sitters Club. Children and mysteries our specialty."

Then the phone rang and we settled down to business.

Until the next mystery, I thought, looking fondly around the room at my fellow BSC members. And I didn't have any doubts that there would be one. Not if I knew the Baby-sitters Club.

L. GODWIN

Ann M. Martin

About the Author

ANN MATTHEWS MARTIN was born on August 12, 1955. She grew up in Princeton, NJ, with her parents and her younger sister, Jane.

Although Ann used to be a teacher and then an editor of children's books, she's now a full-time writer. She gets the ideas for her books from many different places. Some are based on personal experiences. Others are based on childhood memories and feelings. Many are written about contemporary problems or events.

All of Ann's characters, even the members of the Baby-sitters Club, are made up. (So is Stoneybrook.) But many of her characters are based on real people. Sometimes Ann names her characters after people she knows, other times she chooses names she likes.

In addition to the Baby-sitters Club books, Ann Martin has written many other books for children. Her favorite is *Ten Kids, No Pets* because she loves big families and she loves animals. Her favorite Baby-sitters Club book is *Kristy's Big Day*. (By the way, Kristy is her favorite baby-sitter!)

Ann M. Martin now lives in New York with her cats, Gussie and Woody. Her hobbies are reading, sewing, and needlework — especially making clothes for children.

100 (and more)
Reasons to Stay Friends Forever!

More titles... ➧

The Baby-sitters Club titles continued...

Available wherever you buy books...or use this order form.
Scholastic Inc., P.O. Box 7502, 2931 E. McCarty Street, Jefferson City, MO 65102

Please send me the books I have checked above. I am enclosing $_____
(please add $2.00 to cover shipping and handling). Send check or money order–
no cash or C.O.D.s please.

Name_____ Birthdate_____

Address _____

City_____ State/Zip _____